Harvey and Macdougal stood side by side, staring at each other.

Both appeared a little dazed. But thank goodness they both looked all right. Neither had turned into a frog or a pineapple or a toilet bowl brush.

But how in the world could she explain the magic zap, sparkling sprinkles, and purple smoke?

Sabrina ran up to Harvey and laid her hands on his shoulders. "Harvey!" she whispered, searching his big brown eyes. "Are you all right?"

Harvey scratched at his ear with his hand, shook his head a little, and then uttered a single word that sent chills down Sabrina's spine.

"Woof!"

Then Harvey said, "Sabrina . . . what happened?"
But the words didn't come out of Harvey's mouth.
They came out of the dog's mouth!

Sabrina, the Teenage Witch™ books

Available from Archway Paperbacks

A Dog's Life

Cathy East Dubowski

AN ARCHWAY PAPERBACK
Published by POCKET BOOKS
New York London Toronto Sydney Tokyo Singapore

AN ARCHWAY PAPERBACK *Original*

An Archway Paperback published by
POCKET BOOKS, a division of Simon & Schuster Inc.
1230 Avenue of the Americas, New York, NY 10020

ISBN: 0-671-01979-1

First Archway Paperback printing April 1998

10 9 8 7 6 5 4

AN ARCHWAY PAPERBACK and colophon are registered trademarks of Simon & Schuster Inc.

Printed in the U.S.A.

IL: 5+

To the real Macdougal,
who keeps us safe
and loves us as we are

A Dog's Life

☆

Chapter 1

☆

Whack!

Splat!

"Darn!" Sabrina Spellman glared at the busted egg yolk staring back at her from the mixing bowl. Her grandmother's recipe for black walnut fudge brownies called for three eggs—but that *didn't* include chunks of the shell.

She flipped her blond hair over her shoulder and leaned over the bowl to pick out the little white shards.

Maybe I'm trying too hard, she thought. After all, she was trying to make these brownies the old-fashioned way, just the way her mortal grandmother used to do.

By hand.

But trying to pick eggshell out of gooey egg was too hard, and a little icky, and besides, hadn't their consumer's education teacher just warned them that you could get sick from raw eggs if they were contaminated with the bacteria salmonella?

"Sorry, Granny," Sabrina said aloud. "Gotta do this part the Spellman way."

She stared at the egg.

> *"Bits of shell and goo, I beg—*
> *Please gather back into an uncracked egg."*

Magic sparkles shot from Sabrina's pointed fingertip and swirled round the bowl. A sound like the strumming of a tiny fairy's harp danced through the air.

Instantly the egg yolk and all the broken pieces of shell rose from the bowl and hovered before Sabrina's face. Like a video running backward, the broken yolk re-formed into a perfect yellow circle. The fragments of eggshell revolved around it like the planets round the sun. The magic sparkles twinkled like miniature stars.

Sabrina made a little scooting motion with her fingers, and the egg tucked itself into the largest piece of shell. The broken pieces came together like the pieces of a jigsaw puzzle. And then all the cracks healed.

"Very nice, Sabrina," Aunt Zelda called out as she hurried into the kitchen. Sabrina's slender blond aunt snapped her fingers and instantly changed her casual shirt and pants into an elegant turquoise business suit.

2

Sabrina smiled proudly and plucked the perfect white egg from the air. "Thanks."

She hadn't always been able to *un*crack eggs. Up until her sixteenth birthday she'd been as average as the next girl.

That's when she'd come to live with her dad's sisters—Aunt Zelda and Aunt Hilda—in West-bridge, Massachusetts.

And that's when she'd learned that there was something different about her. Something special.

Something *magical.*

Sabrina Spellman was a witch.

Well, half witch anyway. Her dad and her aunts and everyone on their side of the family were witches. But her mother was mortal. And doing things the mortal way sometimes made her feel closer to her mom.

"Now," she said, holding the egg over the bowl. "Let's try this again."

"But why bother at all?" asked Aunt Hilda, bouncing down the stairs. She wound up her arm like a baseball pitcher and pointed toward the kitchen bar.

Ka-BOOM! No one jumped at the tiny explosion that sounded like an oven blowing up. And when the purplish-black smoke cleared, a huge platter of double fudge brownies appeared on the counter.

"Chocolate attacks *can't* wait." Hilda's dimples showed as she stuffed a huge gooey brownie into her mouth. "Ohhh! They are absolutely the *best* I've *ever* made. Want one, Zelda?"

"Well . . . maybe just a teensy one," her sister replied. But first she zapped a china dessert plate and a linen napkin into her hand.

Hilda floated the platter of brownies over to her niece. "Here you go, Sabrina—fresh baked with no waiting."

"But that's not the point," Sabrina insisted. "I want to make these on my own."

Hilda frowned, puzzled. "I made *these* on my own. You can, too. It's in the recipe section of your *Discovery of Magic* book. Page 505."

"But I mean with my whole *hands,*" Sabrina explained. "Not just my *finger.* And with bowls and pans and ovens and stuff."

"But why?" both aunts wanted to know.

"Perhaps it's a school project," Zelda guessed.

"No, it's not for school," Sabrina said as she tried to get up the nerve to crack the egg again. "You know I love being a witch. I love having magic powers, and I'm glad I'm finally learning all these things I never knew about Dad's side of the family. And I'm proud to carry on the Spellman tradition of learning how to use my magic. But sometimes . . . well, I am half-mortal. And I feel I owe it to my mom to keep up some of *her* family's traditions, too. Like cooking the old-fashioned way."

Hilda folded her arms and gave Sabrina a look. "I don't remember your mother cooking," she said. "Do you, Zelda?"

"Anyone can learn how to cook," Zelda said

diplomatically. "Sabrina, your mother has many other fine talents."

"True," Sabrina admitted.

Her mother was a brilliant, passionate archaeologist who had never really been into the Martha-Stewart-beautiful-living kind of stuff. Right now she was somewhere in Peru crawling around in the dirt, digging up remnants of some lost civilization—and, Sabrina was certain, loving every minute of it.

Sabrina hadn't seen her in ages because of this weird witch rule: If Sabrina laid eyes on her mother anytime during the two years following her sixteenth birthday, something bad would happen to her mother.

She'd instantly turn into a ball of wax. Definitely not a way to get on your mother's good side! Sabrina's aunts had explained it was the way the Witches' Council discouraged marriages between witches and mortals.

And that's why she was here, now, living with her aunts in Westbridge. They were entrusted with the dubious honor of training her to use her new magical powers during these two very important years.

"But I haven't seen her since before I turned into a witch," Sabrina argued. "And when I see her again, well . . . I want her to know I'm still her daughter—the same old me. I don't want her to think I'm weird."

"Listen, Sabrina, if your mother thought witches

5

were weird, she never would have married your father," Hilda pointed out.

That was true. But Sabrina worried that maybe it was the differences between the mortal world and the witch world that had led to her parents' divorce. And she didn't want those differences to come between her and her mother.

"You guys can understand, can't you?" Sabrina asked wistfully. "I'm not like most witches. I'm half-mortal. I belong to both worlds."

Zelda's eyes misted a little as she gave Sabrina a quick hug. "You're right, sweetheart. I guess sometimes we get so caught up in our own realm, we forget. I think it's wonderful that you feel that way about your mother and her family. A lot of girls in your situation might have rejected the mortal world outright once they got a little magic in the fingertips."

Sabrina smiled. She knew Aunt Zelda would understand.

With renewed determination, she turned back to her cooking—and that frustrating egg.

"Now, what was it that Granny used to say . . ." she mumbled.

"Don't be a chicken, Sabrina! Smack the egg sharply on the side of the bowl. Hold the egg with your thumbs along the crack. Then open the egg as if you were opening a book."

Do it, Sabrina! she told herself.

Crack!

Plop!

6

Perfect! Only egg dropped into the bowl this time. She repeated the process with the second and third eggs. "See?" she exclaimed excitedly. "I'm doing it!"

Hilda wrinkled her nose. "Yuck. Looks messy to me." She picked up the platter of brownies. "Sure you don't want these?"

"No, thanks."

Hilda shrugged. Then she shrunk the platter down to the size of a doll's plate, zapped a plastic sandwich bag around it, and tucked it into her black velvet shoulder bag. "Have it your way. I'll just take these with me."

"Why do I get the feeling you guys are leaving?" Sabrina asked, reaching over to turn down the volume on the boom box she'd brought into the kitchen. WTTW was giving away advance copies of the new Leopard Spots CD and she wanted to be the lucky thirteenth caller.

"I'm sorry, Sabrina," Zelda said. "Didn't we tell you? I've got an emergency meeting with the Witches' Council this evening, and I'm dragging Hilda along with me to take notes."

"Will you be okay by yourself?" Hilda asked.

"Sure," Sabrina said. She picked up her mixing spoon as if she were about to do battle. "I'm going to a mixer."

Hilda shrugged as she tossed a glittering shawl around her shoulders. "Whatever rings your chimes!" she said with a smile that said she definitely didn't understand. Then she headed up the polished wooden stairs to the second floor. The Spellman sisters had a shortcut to the Other Realm through the upstairs linen closet. "Hey, Zelda, we'd better get going. Want me to hold the door for you?"

"I'm coming!" Zelda called out, running toward the stairs. But suddenly she stopped and spun around. She took a few steps toward the dining room, then stopped again to zap a large antique-looking hourglass in front of her eyes. "Oh, dear!" she exclaimed, obviously torn. "Look at the time!

"Sabrina, darling, could you do me a *big* favor? I'm late as it is. You see, I got so involved with my latest experiment I lost track of time. Would you be a dear and clean up the Lab-Top for me? I just hate to leave such a mess till morning."

Sabrina's aunts had recently come into a huge sum of money when one of their investment bonds from the year 1660 matured. Hilda had wanted to blow it on fun stuff, but Zelda had insisted on investing most of it in a sensible Lab-Top chemistry laboratory.

Closed, the Lab-Top looked something like a large, flat, aluminum suitcase or portfolio. But opened, it looked more like the laboratory of Merlin the Magician—if he'd worked his magic in the year 2000. Its sleek, high-tech laboratory equipment bubbled and smoked with eerie purple and toad-green liquids and mysterious powders, combining the best magic of witches' potions with the latest in modern science.

Her aunt was so proud of it. Zelda Spellman was not only a witch but also a brilliant theoretical chemical physicist with degrees from M.I.T. and Cal Tech. And she had a strong desire to use her brains for something good. With the Lab-Top she believed she might one day make her mark with a scientific discovery that would truly benefit the entire cosmos. Or at least everyone on Earth.

"Sure, Aunt Zelda, I'll take care of it," Sabrina said distractedly as she disposed of the shells.

"Thanks, dear!" With a cheery wave, she dashed up the stairs.

A moment later lightning flashed. Thunder shook the old Victorian house.

Sabrina knew that her aunts had disappeared through the linen closet's neat stack of sheets and towels. In two blinks they'd be in the Other Realm—not bad for a trip that was ten million light-years away.

Sabrina turned back to her grandmother's worn cookbook and ran her fingertip down the instructions.

Gurgle—erp!
Whooooosh!

She could hear the gentle gurgling and burping of chemicals from the Lab-Top in the nearby dining room. She knew she ought to get in there now and clean up. But she really wanted to get these brownies in the oven first. "As soon as I finish this . . ."

"Can I lick the bowl when you're done?" an old-lady voice called out.

Sabrina turned to the old portrait hanging in an antique frame on the kitchen wall. The stern-looking woman in the painting wore her dark hair pulled back into a severe bun, and her prim black dress was topped with a lace collar fastened at her throat with a cameo pin. But this wasn't your ordinary painting of an ancestor—this one talked back.

"But, Aunt Louisa," Sabrina warned the painting, "you'll get chocolate on your frame."

"Oh, nuts," Louisa complained. "I never have any fun." Then her eyes popped open wide. "Nuts! Don't forget the nuts! I love brownies with nuts. Brownies without nuts are like a black cat without whiskers."

Sabrina pointed—the old-fashioned way—at her cutting board. "Black walnuts. Will that do?"

"Awesome!" Aunt Louisa squealed.

"I'll save you a brownie," Sabrina told her.

Sabrina turned back to her cookbook. *Let's see . . . Add one teaspoon baking powder.* Now, where did her aunts keep that? She opened the secret spice cabinet that her aunts kept behind Aunt Louisa's portrait and poked around among the colored bottles, cans, and jars. No luck. Nothing but dried eye of newt, rare herbs, and a multitude of other mysterious ingredients that the Spellman sisters used to concoct potions and brews. She closed Aunt Louisa's portrait, then began to search the rest of the kitchen cabinets.

Just then the front doorbell rang. Sabrina wiped

her hands on a dish towel and hurried to the foyer. When she opened the huge oak door, her heart did a funny flip-flop.

Harvey Kinkle stood in her doorway, his grin as crooked as always, and looking as adorable as a puppy.

When Sabrina was new to Westbridge, she'd immediately developed a crush on Harvey. After a while they'd started dating. In fact, Sabrina had believed he was her one true love. But relationships don't always have fairy-tale endings, even when you're a teenage witch with magic powers at your fingertips. Somehow the world had come between them: football, and parents, and algebra, and schoolwork had torn them apart. Plus all the grown-ups kept saying it was better for them not to get too serious at their age.

But they'd been through too much together— and liked each other way too much—not to remain good friends. Who knew? There was still plenty of time for that fairy-tale ending.

"Hey, Harvey. Whatya doing?"

Harvey grinned. "Walking the dog."

"But you don't have a dog."

Woof!

Sabrina glanced down by Harvey's feet. "You *do* have a dog!" A beautiful reddish golden retriever sat panting at Harvey's side.

"Oh, he's adorable," Sabrina squealed. "Did you just get him?"

"No, I wish!" Harvey bent over and gave the dog

a thorough scratching along the back of its head. "You know Mr. and Mrs. Milligen who live next door to me?"

"You mean the couple who wear those matching bowling shirts wherever they go?"

Harvey nodded. "This is their dog. I'm dog-sitting for them while they're away. They went to this major regional bowling tournament in Boston. They even talked my mom and dad into going with them."

"So it's just you and the dog?"

"Yeah. Pretty cool, huh?"

Sabrina bent down to look the dog in the eyes. "What's his name?"

"Macdougal," Harvey said. "It's a Scottish name. I read that golden retrievers were originally bred as Scottish hunting dogs, and they . . ."

Harvey stopped and sniffed the air.

Sabrina stared at him. "Uh . . . Harvey?"

"Something sure smells good." He sniffed again. "Smells like . . . chocolate. With nuts."

"Harvey Kinkle, I can't believe you!" Sabrina exclaimed. "I'm making brownies, but I haven't even put them in the oven yet. How could you tell?"

Harvey shrugged. "I dunno. I just have a good nose, I guess." He chuckled. "Maybe that's why Macdougal and I get along so well."

"Well, come on in," she invited him. "I'm just about to put them in the oven."

Harvey hesitated on the threshold. "You sure your aunts won't mind?"

"Of course not. They like you."

"I meant, you know—the dog."

"Oh." Sabrina smiled at Macdougal and shook her head. "Nah. We're used to animals in the house around here."

Sabrina led Harvey and Macdougal into the huge comfortable living room.

"Sit," Harvey commanded softly. He grinned when Macdougal immediately obeyed.

"Isn't he just so cool?" Harvey said. "Man, I wish he was my dog. I tell you, Sabrina, dogs have got the life! Walking, hanging out, eating, running around, eating some more . . ."

Sabrina decided not to point out that most dogs could learn to sit on command. What harm would it do to let Harvey think Macdougal was a genius?

"Shake," Harvey said next. And he was nearly ecstatic when the dog placed his paw in the boy's hand.

"If this were my dog," Harvey said, admiring the animal, "I'd enter him in a dog show tomorrow."

"Oh, that reminds me," Sabrina said. "I've got that new Man Bites Dog CD. You want to hear it?"

"Cool."

"I'll go get it. I'll be right back."

Sabrina ran up the long wooden staircase, but stopped with her hand on the railing.

The dining room! She hadn't put the Lab-Top away. What if Harvey saw it?

I could tell him it's just a high-tech chemistry set, she thought. But just in case . . .

"Hey, Harv?"

"Yeah?"

"It doesn't really matter or anything, but maybe you should keep Macdougal out of the dining room. It's—"

What?

"—kind of a mess in there."

"Sure. No problem." He laughed. "That's what my mom does when company comes—shoves the mess into one room and closes the door."

She could hear Harvey practicing tricks with Macdougal in the hallway between the front door and the kitchen as she hurried upstairs. She couldn't help but grin. Harvey was kind of like a sweet, lovable dog himself.

Sabrina ran to her room, but as soon as she dashed through the doorway, she skidded to a stop.

Salem, her black cat, met her with an icy stare.

"What?" Sabrina asked.

"I smell *dog.*" His nose twitched.

Salem was actually a witch himself, but he'd been caught trying to take over the world and been sentenced by the Witches' Council to live a hundred years as a cat. Without any powers other than the ability to talk to humans.

And annoy them.

Sabrina popped her stereo open and removed a CD, which she slipped into a disc sleeve. "Harvey's dog-sitting for this really cool dog named Macdougal," she said with a teasing look in her eye. "Want to go meet him?"

"Yeah, right," Salem drawled. He shuddered as if he'd just swallowed a hairball.

Sabrina hurried downstairs and handed the disc case to Harvey, then frowned.

"What's wrong?" Harvey asked.

"I grabbed the wrong case. This is *Mozart's Greatest Hits.*"

She didn't mention it was an original recording of Mozart himself—in concert!—that her aunts had recorded themselves during the musical genius's "Feel the Heat" tour. Witches had CD technology way before humans did.

"I didn't know you were into classical music," Harvey commented.

Sabrina shrugged. "Aunt Zelda read somewhere that listening to Mozart does something to your brain waves to make you smarter, so I decided to try it when I study."

After all, Aunt Zelda had studied while Mozart played, and look how smart she was. Of course, she'd had front-row seats.

"Maybe I should try it," Harvey said. "Only . . . well, I like classical music, but most of the time it just puts me to sleep."

"Don't worry," Sabrina told him. "Man Bites Dog will *really* wake you up! You've got to see these lyrics. I'll be right back. You can crank up my CD player. It's in the kitchen."

"Okay."

Sabrina ran back upstairs while Harvey headed for the kitchen with Macdougal following close on his heels. He popped in the CD and pressed "Play."

Nothing.

He pressed it again.

Nothing again.

"Hmmm," he said aloud with a shrug. "Maybe the batteries are dead." Without checking the volume, he popped open the back of the player, extracted the cord and turned toward the counter. He looked around, but he couldn't find an empty outlet. Figuring Sabrina wouldn't be making toast anytime soon with brownies in the works, he shrugged and unplugged a cord. Then he plugged in the CD player.

When Sabrina came back down, the music was blasting, Harvey and the dog were playing, and the oven was beeping to let her know it was preheated. "Time to get these puppies going. Oops! Sorry, Macdougal."

"Don't worry," Harvey said, wrestling a tennis ball away from the dog. "He's pretty easygoing about that stuff. Dog days of summer, Three Dog Night . . ."

Sabrina picked up the hand mixer and stuck the blades into the thick batter. She flipped the switch.

Nothing happened.

"Uh, I probably ought to take Macdougal out for a walk soon," Harvey said. "He's getting a little jumpy."

So was Sabrina. Why wouldn't the mixer start?

And wait—she'd completely forgotten about the baking powder. She couldn't find it in any of the cabinets. What if her aunts didn't have any?

Sabrina fumed. What had started out as a fun project for a lonely evening was turning into a chore. And now that it wasn't such a lonely evening—now that Harvey was here—she just wanted to get the brownies in the oven and be done with it.

Maybe I could just take a tiny little shortcut, she thought. *Surely Granny wouldn't mind.*

Sabrina glanced over her shoulder.

Harvey was busy doing tricks with Macdougal. He wouldn't notice if she did a little quick witchery.

Turning back to the brownies, she raised her finger and prepared to zap it with first a substitution spell, to add her own generic brand of baking powder, then a mixing spell, since the mixer had bailed on her.

> *"Listen well to this little witch,*
> *Take this and this and make a switch.*
> *Mix it up until you're done,*
> *Make it great for everyone."*

Sabrina had to admit it was one of her lamest rhymes yet, but she was hungry and she wanted to go hang out with Harvey.

But as she flicked her wrist to give it the proper mixing swirl, Harvey yelled.

"No! Macdougal! Not in the dining room!"

The dining room!

Without hesitating Sabrina turned.

And so did her hand.

But the spell had already been unleashed from within her, and it shot forward, completely missing the mixing bowl . . .

Bounced off the shiny surface of the toaster—*Ping!*

And whomped Harvey as he ducked through the doorway chasing Macdougal . . .

Just as Macdougal smashed into the Lab-Top . . .

Crash!

Splash!

Zap! Woof! Ka-ZING!

Boy and dog lit up like Christmas lights and fireworks on the Fourth of July combined.

Sabrina gasped. Her hands flew to her face, covering her eyes.

Oh, no. What have I done?

In the year since she'd come to live with her aunts, Sabrina had learned that the powerful magic of witches could be dangerous and have unexpected results even when used carefully. But out-of-control magic . . . *whoa!*

Sabrina shivered. She didn't want to look.

At last she made herself peek through her fingers.

Harvey and Macdougal stood side by side, staring at each other. Both appeared a little dazed. But thank goodness they both looked all right. Neither had turned into a frog or a pineapple or a toilet bowl brush.

But how in the world could she explain the magic zap, sparkling sprinkles, and purple smoke?

Sabrina ran up to Harvey and laid her hands on his shoulders. "Harvey!" she whispered, searching his big brown eyes. "Are you all right?"

Harvey scratched at his ear with his hand, shook his head a little, and then uttered a single word that sent chills down Sabrina's spine.

"Woof!"

Then Harvey said, "Sabrina . . . what happened?"

But the words didn't come out of Harvey's mouth.

They came out of the dog's mouth!

Sabrina felt faint.

Doggone it!

Her substitution-mixing spell had gotten totally mixed up.

Harvey and Macdougal had switched bodies!

Chapter 2

☆

☆

"Arr-Arr-Arr-Arr-Arr-Arr!"

Macdougal—or Harvey—the dog yelped and ran under the baby grand piano in the living room. He cowered there, whimpering as if he'd been struck.

"Oh, Harvey! How could I do this to you?" Sabrina wailed. Quickly she got down on her hands and knees and peered under the piano. The dog stared back, the whites showing around his huge brown eyes.

Sabrina gulped. "Harvey?" she asked slowly.

"Arr—*right!*" Sabrina heard Harvey say. But, wait—the words *weren't* coming out of the dog's mouth.

Sabrina's head whipped around and she stared at Harvey—at least, what *looked* like Harvey—standing in the middle of the room, examining his arms and legs as if he'd never seen them before.

"Macdougal?" Sabrina said worriedly.

"Woof!" the dog replied in Harvey's voice. "Digit!" Then he grinned, panting, with his tongue hanging out.

Yikes! This is really *weird.* Macdougal the dog was inside Harvey's body. But instead of barking, he was talking in Harvey's voice, only a little more . . . well, deep and growly.

"Is that you, Macdougal?" Sabrina asked, hoping the whole thing was a crazy dream.

Macdougal nodded Harvey's head enthusiastically. "Mmm-hmmm."

"But how can you talk?" she asked.

Macdougal pawed at Harvey's head right behind Harvey's left ear. "Dunno," he muttered. He ran Harvey's fingertips over Harvey's face, seemingly amazed at the new words spilling forth. "Just think it," he grunted, "and it comes out."

Sabrina had seen some awfully weird things since coming to live in Westbridge with her supernatural aunts. But she wasn't prepared for this. Macdougal the dog inside Harvey's body. And the dog's thoughts taking place in Harvey's brain were coming out of Harvey's mouth. And somehow, whatever knowledge, whatever vocabulary that was stored in the computer banks of Harvey's brain, the dog had access to.

So he could talk. The *dog* could talk.

Two years of living with Salem the talking cat wasn't enough to prepare her for a dog talking through the mouth of one of her best friends!

And what about Harvey—the *real* Harvey?

Sabrina turned back to the reddish-brown dog and looked anxiously into his eyes. "Harvey? Harvey, can you hear me?"

At first Harvey the dog just scooted farther back under the piano with a terrified look on his face.

What if Harvey was trapped inside the dog's body—but couldn't speak? What if he couldn't understand Sabrina? How frightened would he be?

"Harvey," Sabrina repeated gently. "Do you under-stand me?"

"Yeah," Harvey gasped through his sharp doggie teeth. "But . . . but Sabrina! I *don't* . . . understand. What's . . ." He struggled to get the words out. ". . . happening?"

"You can talk, too?"

"Course!" he said. "I just can't—Yip! Yip!—stand on two legs!"

Sabrina's mind whirled.

She could only guess that the knowledge and vocabulary in Harvey's spirit—or whatever it was that had transferred from boy body to dog body—was able to make the dog do what evolution had not yet taught it to do: talk.

True, he sounded a little rough, not much better than the dog on that Christmas record she'd once heard on the radio, the one where somebody had taught a dog to "sing" the words to "Jingle Bells."

He looked up at her with frightened brown eyes.

This is probably the scariest thing that has ever happened to him, Sabrina thought. *Next to that time he had to sing "Blue Christmas" at the mall's chorus concert. And it's all my fault.*

What in the world am I going to tell him? she wondered frantically. She could explain away magic sparkles and things that moved by magic. She could usually come up with some kind of explanation when one of her friends accidentally wandered into the witch world of extraordinary happenings.

But how could she explain this to Harvey when it wasn't just some brief, unimportant event? When he was *right* in the middle of it? When he knew without any doubt that he'd somehow turned into a dog?

"Arf," Harvey moaned. "Sabrina, tell me . . . I'm dreaming."

You go, Harvey! Sabrina thought. *Excellent idea!*

"Harvey," Sabrina said firmly and with confidence. "You're dreaming."

"No, I'm not."

"Huh?"

"I know I'm not . . . dreaming."

"How come?" Sabrina asked. "How can you be sure?"

"'Cause," he yelped. "The only thing I *ever* dream about is *sports!*"

"Uh, maybe you're dreaming you're a hunting dog?" Sabrina tried lamely.

Harvey barked. "I don't think so."

"Hey, Harvey," Sabrina heard Macdougal say over her shoulder. "Want *me* to take *you* for a walk? Arf, arf, arf!"

"Macdougal!" Sabrina snapped. "Heel!"

Macdougal the teenage boy obediently sat on his haunches at Sabrina's side.

It made Harvey look ridiculous.

"I told you he was well-trained," Harvey muttered.

Thank heaven for small miracles, Sabrina thought.

Now, what can I do? Think, Sabrina! she told herself. Would she have to make up a new spell? Or just reverse the spell she'd originally cast? Maybe if she—

"Sabrina?" Harvey the dog suddenly whined.

"Yeah, Harvey?"

"I'm starting to freak."

"Don't freak!" Sabrina shrieked.

But it was too late.

He freaked.

Harvey the dog started racing around the living room as if he were trying to escape his own skin. He crashed into tables. He knocked over an ancient vase that her aunts had brought back from a Marco Polo tour of China in the year 1275. Fortunately Sabrina managed to catch that with a freeze-frame spell and put it up on the mantel where it couldn't get broken. Then he slipped on a throw rug and went sliding across the polished wood floor of the entry hall—*crash!*—into the front door.

Poor dog! "Harvey! Harvey! Come here, boy!" Sabrina called. She clapped and whistled for him the way she'd call any dog. *"Fwee-wheet!"*

Instantly Macdougal the boy jumped up on her and put his arms on her shoulders. Then he starting licking her face!

"Harvey!" she shrieked. "I mean—Macdougal! Quit it right—ewwww, yuck!" It was like Harvey slobbering all over her face—only he was doing it the way a goofy, overly affectionate dog would.

"Stop!" she squealed as they tumbled to the carpeted floor. "This is *too weird!*"

Suddenly she heard laughter coming from the stairs.

Sabrina shoved Harvey, or Macdougal—or whoever he was!—to the side and glared darts at Salem Saberhagen. Soon-to-be-an-"outside" cat Salem.

"It's not funny, Salem!"

"Oh, but you're wrong," Salem crowed, laughing so hard he had to wipe tears from his eyes with his little black paw. "It's hilarious."

"How would you like to be a *stuffed* cat for the next hundred years?" Salem threatened as she got to her feet.

"Now, now, Sabrina, calm down," Salem said as he watched Harvey the dog continue to race around the room. Clearly Harvey was too preoccupied to notice Sabrina was talking to her cat, who was talking back. Then the cat's eyes lit up.

"Video!"

"Huh?"

"Get the video camera!" Salem cried. "We'll put this on one of those funniest-home-video shows. We'll be rich!"

Sabrina rolled her eyes. "Is that all you ever think about—money?"

Salem swished his tail in thought. "Hmm. It's third, actually. After power and tuna."

Thump! Sabrina groaned as she felt Macdougal tackle her for another slobberfest.

"Sit!" she commanded, and the hound in boy's clothing instantly sat.

On the floor.

Sabrina sighed. "It's *okay* to sit on the couch now, Macdougal."

"Arr-*right!*" He jumped on the couch with a blissful look on his face.

Sabrina turned her attention back to Harvey the dog just in time to catch a delicate glass figurine—a gift to Aunt Zelda from Louis XVI—from smashing to the floor. She floated it to the mantel beside the Chinese vase. Then, before she did anything else, she muttered under her breath so Harvey wouldn't hear—not that the crazy dog boy was paying any attention to her at the moment!

"All things fragile, all antiques, too,
Ignore bumps and jostles and stick like glue."

She waved her arms, and a brief sound like the strumming of a harp breezed through the room.

She tested a lamp on a side table. It wouldn't budge. Good. Now she could get down to business.

"Harvey!" Sabrina commanded, clapping her hands. "Come here."

But the boy-dog was too upset to obey.

Sabrina tried to catch him, but he was a big, strong dog, and he wriggled free.

Sabrina frowned. Then she snapped her fingers and a brand-new box of Yum-Yum Doggie Biscuits for Large Dogs appeared in her hand.

"Oh, Har-vey," Sabrina sang out. "Want a cookie?"

The dog screeched to a halt and sat up, begging for a doggie treat.

"Good dog!" Sabrina said and gave him one of the ten-inch-long, bone-shaped snacks. Immediately he sank to the floor with the tasty treat between his front paws and began to chew.

Sabrina stroked the soft, reddish-brown dog from his forehead down along his back. "Poor Harvey," she cooed. "It's okay. Everything's going to be all right."

The teenage boy in him suddenly stopped short and stared at the bone in front of him with a mixture of shock and disgust. "What am I doing?" he gasped. "I'm eating a doggie bone!"

But then his dog instincts took over and he shrugged. "Whatever." Then he happily went back to munching his snack.

That was Harvey. Smart, but not too complicated. Innocent and trusting. Took life as it came, without asking too many questions.

Maybe that will work in my favor, Sabrina thought.

"Now, listen carefully," Sabrina said, sitting cross-legged beside him on the floor. "I'll explain everything."

"This ought to be good," Salem snickered from his perch on the stair.

"Hush, Salem!" Sabrina thought hard for a moment. What *could* she tell him?

It seemed as if there were no way out.

Maybe it's time, she thought. Maybe it was time to finally share her secret, to tell someone that she was a witch with magic powers beyond anything most humans could possibly imagine. Far beyond what she herself had imagined only a couple of years ago.

And Harvey—if she trusted anyone to be loyal and not tell secrets, it was good old, reliable, honest Harvey.

What else could she do?

She opened her mouth to tell him . . .

☆

Chapter 3

☆

Sabrina hesitated.

She pictured her aunts' faces when they found out she'd told. Her aunts wouldn't like it. And it would complicate things immensely.

And what if, somehow, it did get out? What if Harvey accidentally let it slip to someone not so trustworthy.

Somebody like Libby—head cheerleader and school blabbermouth—who hated Sabrina's guts?

That could actually put Aunt Zelda and Aunt Hilda in danger.

Then she imagined the Quizmaster shaking his head at her and moaning, "Sabrina, Sabrina, Sabrina . . . if you'd only studied page 347 of your Handbook—"

"All right, all right!" she mumbled, waving her

hand in front of her face as if to chase away the critical images. "I won't tell!"

She sighed and glanced around the old Victorian house that she'd come to think of as home, as if somehow its walls could give her the answer.

She headed into the kitchen to get Macdougal— er, Harvey—a bowl of water.

"What do I do now?" Sabrina sighed as she turned on the faucet.

"Psst!" Aunt Louisa whispered from her framed portrait on the wall. "Take 'em both to the pound!"

Aunt Louisa! Sabrina mouthed, glaring sternly and putting her finger to her lips.

Aunt Louisa cackled softly, but then resumed her serious pose.

Sabrina filled a cereal bowl with cool water, then carried it back into the living room.

Then Sabrina's eyes wandered to the dining room door. Inside she could see the Lab-Top that she'd failed to clean up as she'd promised, now an even bigger mess. The broken test tubes, the purple and pink spills. The pungent smells . . .

And suddenly her face brightened. "That's it!" she cried.

Harvey the dog looked up from the crumbs of his doggie cookie.

Even Macdougal the boy quit playing with his new opposable thumb for a moment to lean forward with interest.

"Harvey," Sabrina addressed her friend. "Everything's going to be all right. But you have to promise that whatever I tell you, you'll keep it a secret."

Harvey looked troubled, but he said, "All right."

"You, too, Macdougal."

"Woof."

Sabrina took a deep breath. "Well, Harvey, you know my aunt Zelda is a scientific genius. And she's been doing some top-secret research."

"Mmm-hmm."

"Well, you know the chemicals from my aunt's lab set that spilled all over you guys when Macdougal crashed into the dining room table?"

"Yeah."

"Well, this is very top secret," Sabrina whispered, "but I'm afraid the chemical caused some kind of hyperactive molecular transference—"

"What?"

"—combined with the extrasensory perception factor—you do believe in ESP, don't you?"

"I think so."

"Within your, um, west cerebral hemisphere creating an, er, out-of-body-experience type of transfer between you and Macdougal, with whom you share certain psychic sympathies and connections."

"Huh?"

Harvey was not all that great in regular biology and chemistry. With a great deal of effort he could usually post a strong C, if he was lucky. But maybe that would help her story even more. Since he wasn't a scientific genius, he wouldn't be able to challenge the factual accuracy of her totally bogus scientific explanation.

"Well," Sabrina said as seriously as possible, "I'll spare you all the scientific theory and mumbo-jumbo. But it's very hush-hush. Can I trust you to keep it secret?"

"I . . . I don't know, Sabrina, I guess so," Harvey said. He stopped to scratch his ear with his back paw. "As long as you can fix it."

"Fix it?" Sabrina squeaked. She gave him a forced smile. "Of course—"

"Okay."

"Okay, what?"

"Do it. Fix us back."

"Now?"

"Why not?"

"Well, um, I can't right now," Sabrina said, searching her mind for an explanation. "I have to talk privately with my aunt. She never discusses this in front of anyone. Who knows what might happen if the formula fell into the wrong hands.

"Besides," she added, "weren't you just saying earlier how cool it would be to be a dog?"

"Yeah . . ."

"You said a dog's life must be the—"

"Happiest on the planet," Harvey finished thoughtfully.

"And just think," Sabrina added. "You won't have to go to school or anything till I get you switched back. No homework, no chores, no unfair restrictions. You can do whatever you like."

"Hey," Harvey admitted, "it might be fun. For a little while."

"Great," Sabrina said. "I'm sure we'll get you changed back soon."

Lucky for them Harvey's parents—and Macdougal's owners—were out of town for the week. Surely she'd have them changed back by then.

But what about her aunts?

"Harvey," Sabrina said, "we'd better not let Aunt Zelda know about this yet."

Harvey sat up, worried. "But don't we need her to change me back?"

"I'll explain later, okay?" *As soon as I make something up!*

Sabrina smiled calmly at Harvey and Macdougal—or Macdougal and Harvey, however you wanted to look at it. She pretended that everything was fine. "You guys just sit here and hang out," she said. "I'll be right back."

Smiling and nodding, she got up from the couch, then she dashed to where Salem now sat on the kitchen island, his eyes glittering with delight.

"Charming little fib fest, Sabrina."

Sabrina gulped. "Salem! I am in *soooo* much trouble! You've got to help me! Swear you won't tell Aunt Hilda and Aunt Zelda."

"Well, well, well," Salem purred. "What an interesting situation we're in. You're begging me?" His long black tail swished in feline delight. "Now, how much is your little secret worth to you?"

"Come on, Salem," Sabrina said desperately.

"I'll . . . I'll sign you up for the Seafood of the Month Club."

"Mmm, that's a good start . . ."

"I'll be your slave for a week!"

"Mmmmm. Keep going . . ."

"Salem! Please—anything! Just help me. You know Aunt Hilda and Aunt Zelda have been on my case about being serious about my magic. If they find out how badly I messed up this magic, I'll never hear the end of it! They'll ground me for the next century!"

"Why do they have to know?" Salem asked. "Why don't you just send Harvey and the dog—or is that the other way around? Anyway, why not just send them both home?"

Sabrina thought about that a moment. "That's an idea. His parents aren't home, and neither are Macdougal's owners."

Then a terrible chill washed over her.

"Wait! I can't do that!"

"Why not?" Salem purred. "Out of sight, out of mind."

"Who knows what Macdougal will do with Harvey's body now that he's off his leash?" Sabrina cried. "He might just run away. We might never find him again. Then we wouldn't be able to switch them back. Come on, Salem," Sabrina pleaded. "Just give me a chance to straighten this whole mess out on my own. I'm sure I can do it, but I just need a little time to figure out what to do. Please, please, please?"

Crash! Boom!

Upstairs Sabrina heard the crash and rumble of thunder and lightning as her aunts arrived home through the linen closet.

"Salem!" Sabrina cried, grabbing his tiny black paws. "Please—I'll do anything!"

"All right, all right." The sleek black cat jumped to the floor and stuck his tail in the air. "But you owe me, Sabrina Spellman."

"Oh, thank you, Salem!" Sabrina exclaimed. "You're the best."

Salem shrugged as only cats can do. "I know it."

"Sabrina," Zelda called. "We're home!"

Sabrina headed for the living room, then suddenly froze.

The Lab-Top!

It was still a total wreck!

Chapter 4

☆

☆

Sabrina raced into the dining room and surveyed the damage. She only had a moment—if that much time—to clean up and cover her tracks.

With the speed of a witch pursued, she cleaned up the spills, put all the equipment back in place, and folded the Lab-Top down into its storage place beneath the dining room table.

"Sabrina!" She heard Zelda call out again from the top of the stairs as she used Witchlight Stain Remover to remove the spill from the carpet.

That was way too close! Sabrina thought as she hurried back into the living room.

"Sabrina!" Hilda squealed as she hurried down the stairs. "Wait till you hear about what happened in the Other Realm—"

Both aunts froze in mid-step when they saw someone they knew sitting on the living room

36

couch. Recognizing Harvey, they exchanged glances, then calmly came downstairs.

"The Other Realm?" Harvey in the dog's body asked.

"It's a . . . a restaurant they like to go to," Sabrina whispered.

"I never heard of it."

"It's out of town!" Sabrina said. "Now, shhh! Don't talk anymore. Pretend you're a dog!"

Harvey sat up and laid his front paw on Sabrina's knee. "How's this?" he whispered.

"Good," she said, then caught her aunts watching her out of the corner of her eye. "Good *dog!*" she added, smiling as she patted him on the head.

"Harvey," Zelda said as she sat down on the couch next to the teenage boy in the plain flannel shirt who she thought was the real Harvey. "We haven't seen much of you lately. How have you been?"

Macdougal didn't answer at first. Even though Zelda was staring right at him.

"Harvey," Sabrina said, giving him a nudge with her elbow, "has been real busy lately. Haven't you, *Harvey?"*

"Ruff!" Macdougal said.

Her aunts looked puzzled.

"Really *rough,"* Sabrina agreed, nodding. "School has really been rough lately. So much homework. And of course, Harvey's got sports, too. Who has time for anything. Right, Harvey?"

"Right," Macdougal said from inside Harvey's body.

"Right," Harvey said from inside the dog's body.

Sabrina grabbed another dog biscuit and shoved it in Harvey the dog's mouth. "Here you go, *Macdougal!*" she said pointedly, trying to remind him. "That should keep you busy for a while."

Harvey happily forgot about everything but the tasty treat.

"Can I have one, too?" Macdougal asked, hungrily eyeing the dog treat. "I'm starved."

Zelda and Hilda stared at Sabrina's friend.

Sabrina forced herself to burst out laughing, slapping her knee. "Oh, Harvey, you are *so* funny!"

Her aunts laughed, too.

"Let me see what we've got to eat," Hilda said, hurrying into the kitchen. "Sabrina, didn't you finish your brownies yet?"

"Uh, no, Aunt Hilda. I got a little distracted when Harvey came over."

"I told you you should have just zzzzaaa—" Hilda caught herself in mid-sentence "—um, zapped up a batch using *my* recipe. It's *so* much faster."

"I wish I had," Sabrina muttered. "Oh, how I wish I had."

Hilda opened the refrigerator and blinked. A beautiful apple pie appeared on the empty glass shelf. "I bet you forgot all about this lovely pie I baked this morning," she called out.

"Yeah, I did," Sabrina played along.

"Harvey, care for a slice?"

Macdougal the boy followed his nose to the kitchen and took the beautiful pie from Hilda's hands.

Sabrina managed to grab him just before he stuck his face in it to gobble a bite. "Here, Harvey," she said, removing the pie from his hands. "Let me cut you a big slice. Why don't you get a *fork?*" she suggested.

Macdougal's forehead—Harvey's forehead, that is—wrinkled in thought. "Fork?"

"Never mind. I'll get it," Sabrina said. "Just sit—*on the stool!*" she shouted quickly before he could drop to the floor.

Macdougal perched on the bar stool while Sabrina cut him a slice of pie, then put a fork in his hand. When he stared at it suspiciously, she quickly cut herself a slice and slowly, with great exaggeration, began to eat it with a fork, hoping Macdougal would catch on.

No good. When Macdougal tried to use the fork, it was a complete disaster!

First he missed his mouth.

Then he missed the food as it fell in his lap.

Another forkful flew past his head and landed on the table.

When he finally got pie on the fork and into his mouth, he bit at the food but released the fork.

Luckily Hilda was still bustling about, zapping

up some hot chocolate behind Harvey's back, too distracted to notice his bumbling attempts to feed himself.

"Here, have some cookies," Sabrina said, pulling a new—*really* new—box from the cabinet.

Harvey's lopsided grin appeared. "My favorite," Macdougal said.

"What a lovely dog," Aunt Zelda said from the living room. "Is it a golden retriever?"

Macdougal was obviously too interested in his cookies to answer, so Sabrina spoke for him. "His name's Macdougal. Harvey's dog-sitting for the week."

Zelda scratched him behind the ears. "Well, he's just a sweetheart!" Then she stood up and poked her head into the dining room. "Sabrina!"

Sabrina's heart nearly stopped. "What!"

Zelda laughed as she continued into the kitchen. "I was just going to tell you what a lovely job you did cleaning up the dining room. Thanks, dear."

Sabrina's heart settled back to a normal rhythm. "Uh, no problem."

"Well, after I finish my cocoa, I'm going up for a nice long soak in the tub," Hilda said.

Zelda yawned. "I wish I could call it a night. But I've got some council notes to go over." She crossed to an end table to pick up her portable computer.

It wouldn't budge.

Smiling at Harvey, who was totally occupied with getting his nose into the cookie box, she hurried to her niece's side. "Sabrina," she whispered. "Why is my computer stuck to the table?"

"Oops! Sorry, Aunt Zelda." Sabrina angled herself away from "Harvey" and toward her aunt. "Harvey and I had the CD player blasting and all. We were going to . . . to dance. So I just put a spell on all the good stuff so nothing would, you know, fall or crash or anything."

"Why, that was thoughtful of you, Sabrina," Zelda said quietly. "But could you undo it now? I really have a lot of work to do."

"Sure." Sabrina quickly undid the spell, and her aunt headed for the stairs.

"Good night, Harvey. It was nice to see you again," Zelda called out.

"Um, Aunt Zelda?" Sabrina asked nervously. "Harvey really needs our help."

Zelda turned around, her face wrinkled in concern. "Is everything all right?"

No! Sabrina wanted to shout. *Everything is all messed up, Aunt Zelda—and I need your help to fix it!*

But she knew she'd better figure this one out by herself—and fast.

"You see, Harvey's dog-sitting for Macdougal at his house this week. But his hot water heater is broken. What with his folks out of town and everything, do you think he could stay here—in the guest room—till it's fixed?"

Zelda and Hilda exchanged a glance. They were

old pros at living quietly and successfully among mortals without revealing their secret powers. They'd been doing it for five hundred years! But they had rarely had a mortal as an overnight guest, except of course when Sabrina and her mom used to visit when she was little.

"Please?" Sabrina asked in her most sincere voice.

Zelda and Hilda studied the young man at the kitchen bar. He was totally unaware of any of the conversation.

Zelda smiled. "I'm sure he'll be no trouble at all. We'd be glad to have you, Harvey. As long as it's all right with your parents, of course."

Sabrina jabbed Harvey in the ribs. "Say thank you," she whispered.

"Thank you," Macdougal repeated, then stuffed another cookie in his mouth.

"Poor dear," Aunt Zelda whispered to Hilda. "He must be starving without someone at home to cook for him."

Hilda nodded as she followed Zelda up the stairs. "It'll be nice having a dog around the house for a change," she said, loud enough for Salem to hear.

As soon as they were gone, Sabrina dragged Macdougal away from the food and called Harvey the dog with a quick whistle and a few loud pats on her thigh. "Okay, listen up, guys. You can stay here tonight. If I'm lucky, we'll fix everything tomorrow. Till then, everybody behaves. Got it?"

Macdougal shrugged.

Harvey nodded.

Quickly Sabrina hustled the mixed-up boy and dog upstairs and into the second-floor guest room.

As she dashed back to her own room, she caught Salem peeking around the door from her room.

"Salem!" she said. "Just the cat I was looking for."

"Pinch me—I must be dreaming! Sabrina! What are those . . . those mongrels doing up here?"

"Spending the night."

"Sabrina," Salem hissed. "How could you?"

"I had to, Salem," Sabrina explained. "There was no other way. I've got to keep them both here under strict surveillance until I can figure out what to do."

"That's it!" Salem said, turning tail. "Where's my suitcase? I'm *outta* here!"

"No, you're not," Sabrina said, catching the cat around his middle. "Salem, I need you."

Salem stopped in mid cat-step, and there was a tiny catch in his voice when he said, "Me? You need . . . me?"

Cats, Sabrina thought, shaking her head. *They pretend to be so independent. But deep down they need to be needed, just like the rest of us.*

"Yes, you—Salem Saberhagen. For an important job. Something that no one else can do."

"Well," Salem replied, his interest piqued by the flattery. "I don't exactly care for that word you used—"

"What word?"

Salem grimaced, as much as a cat can grimace. *"Job."*

"Forget *job*. Think of it as a favor. A big favor for your favorite teenage witch."

Salem began to back away. "I have the strangest feeling I ought to *scat* right now."

"Oh, no, you don't!" Sabrina said, scooping him into her arms and heading toward the guest room. "You're on guard duty tonight."

Salem choked as if he were coughing up a hairball. "Say *what?*"

"Somebody has to sleep in the guest room with Harvey and Macdougal tonight," Sabrina explained. "To make sure they don't get loose. To make sure nothing goes wrong."

"Uh-uh. No way, not me," Salem said, bristling. "Haven't you ever heard the expression, 'He who lies down with dogs gets up with fleas'?"

"Harvey's wearing a flea collar."

"Why don't *you* stay in there and keep an eye on them?" Salem said as they neared the offensive room.

"I can't," Sabrina said. "It wouldn't be proper. What would Aunt Zelda and Aunt Hilda say?"

"Too bad," Salem said, "because there's no way I'm sleeping in that room tonight."

Sabrina shrugged. "I don't care if you sleep or not. But you're going in there."

"No!" Salem cried. "You can't make me!"

"Oh, yes, I can," Sabrina said. "I just got an O-mail from Amanda this morning." Amanda was the daughter of Sabrina's cousin Marigold. She was a full witch and spoiled in a way only an immortal child could be.

"But you don't have a computer," Salem charged.

"This is different. O-mail is like e-mail from the Other Realm."

Salem shrugged. "So?"

"She wants to know if she can borrow my kitty-cat to play dress-up with!"

"Yowl!" Salem shrieked. "You can't let her do that to me again, Sabrina! That little girl's not a witch—she's an absolute monster! If she gets her hands on me again, I'll use up all my nine lives in a weekend. Please, Sabrina, I'll do anything—"

"Excellent!" Sabrina paused in front of the guest room door and dumped the black cat on the soft oriental carpet runner that covered the floor. "The only anything I need done is for you to play border patrol for our guests."

If Salem had still had any of his witch powers, Sabrina was sure it would have been raining cats and dogs by now, judging by the black cat's murderous expression. But all he said was, "Fine. But I want this deal in writing!"

"Fine." Sabrina zapped a parchment paper contract into one hand and a black stamp pad into the other. She laid both items on the plush carpet in front of Salem's twitching whiskers.

Salem toyed with the carpet's tasseled fringe for a moment, searching for alternatives. When he could think of nothing, he sighed in a long-suffering way and placed his right paw firmly in the center of the stamp pad. "I have a feeling I'm going to regret this," he muttered. But he pressed his pawtograph on the bottom line.

With a quick swirl of her fingertip, Sabrina dashed her own signature onto the contract, then folded it and stuffed it into her back pocket. "Great. Just remember one thing."

"What?"

"Try not to talk around Harvey. It's going to be tough enough for Harvey's brain to handle that he's switched bodies with a dog. I'd just as soon not have to explain you."

"Don't worry, Sabrina," Salem sneered. "The profound lack of conversational partners will make it easier than you could ever imagine."

As the cat pranced regally into the room, Sabrina stuck her head in the door.

Harvey the dog was curled up in the center of the guest bed. Macdougal the teenage boy lay at the foot of the bed, awkwardly curled up on the floor. "Darn. I can't seem to get comfortable," he muttered.

Sabrina rubbed her temples, which had begun to pound, and went into the well-decorated room long enough to shoo the canine Harvey to the foot of the bed and to show the human Macdougal how to actually get *in* the bed, beneath the soft quilts.

"Whoa!" Macdougal yelped, snuggling into the covers. "Weird."

"Now, Harvey, Macdougal," Sabrina began. "This is our cat Salem. He usually sleeps in here." She dropped her voice. "He likes to think it's *his* room." She knew that must sound weird to anyone who didn't know cats, but neither of her guests questioned it.

"No chasing!" she ordered. "Do I make myself clear?"

Both wandering souls nodded solemnly.

"Good. Well, good night." She pulled the door closed.

Sabrina hurried down the hallway to her own room. She immediately reached for the present her father had given her on her sixteenth birthday: an ancient jewel-encrusted leather book called *The Discovery of Magic.* She also grabbed her Witch's Handbook—which, incidentally, was actually in the shape of an oversized hand—that her aunts had given her on her seventeenth birthday.

She carried both to the center of her bed, then began to study as if Westbridge High's final exams were in the morning.

Sabrina had flunked her first test for the Witch's Learner's Permit because she'd been too busy with other things to study. But after a punishing trip to Witches' Boot Camp (a camp *not* shaped like a boot!), she'd realized that studying her magic wasn't just a matter of pleasing grown-ups or getting some grade on a report card from the Other Realm. It was about her life, her future. If she didn't study hard, she couldn't pass her final exam for her Witch's License. And for that, there was no makeup test, no second chance.

If she failed, she'd lose her powers—forever.

So she'd buckled down and begun to study regularly. She knew that some spells could simply be reversed. Other spells required counterspells or magical antidotes. Still others could be dealt with only by breaking the spell up into its smallest elements—sort of like undoing a baked cake into its ingredients. And then, of course, there were the exceptions, which required a witch to come up with brand-new solutions.

If only she knew what she was dealing with here.

Page after page she read, till her eyes grew heavy and her head spun with information.

Suddenly, on impulse, she flipped her *Discovery of Magic* book to the *S*'s. There it was—the black and white etching of her handsome father, Edward Spellman, with his black hair and mustache and elegant evening clothes, looking like a mysterious magician from the distant past.

"Hello, Sabrina!" he called out cheerfully as the black lines shimmered into a living image. "How are you?" His eyes quickly darkened as he hurried to ask, "Is there anything wrong?"

He looked so worried that in spite of everything, she could only bring herself to say, "Of course not, Dad. I just felt like looking you up to say hi."

"I'm glad you did, sweetheart," he said. But then he looked at his watch. "Isn't it a school night?"

"Well, yes," she admitted.

"Shouldn't you be in bed?"

"I am in bed." She was sitting on her bed.

"Sabrina," her father said sternly. "You know I mean asleep."

"Yeah, well, I was just studying my magic, like a good little witch."

Edward's face burst into a huge grin. "That's my girl! How's it going?"

"Really well," Sabrina said truthfully. "I'll be ready when the time comes."

"Excellent," her father replied. "We're all so proud of you, sweetheart. I know it's not easy having to live in both realms and study all the time. But I know you can do it, sweetheart. I'm rooting for you all the way."

Sabrina smiled at her father with great affection, knowing now that she wasn't going to worry him by telling him that in fact she'd messed up her magic today big-time. And the mess involved a mortal. But it was a boost just to hear him say how much he believed in her.

They talked a few minutes more before Edward insisted that she close the book and get some sleep.

"Good night, Sabrina," her father said, "I love you."

"Love you, too," she whispered as she watched his living image flatten once more into a flat picture printed on a page.

But she didn't go to sleep, not for hours, as she studied her handbook, searching for answers.

* * *

Thump! Sabrina awoke suddenly when her Handbook fell to the floor. She sat up and looked around. She must have fallen asleep studying her magic books for some kind of clue.

She stood in front of her mirror and zapped her wrinkly, day-old clothes into clean jeans and a shimmery, pale green top. Then she dashed down the hall to the guest room to check on her menagerie.

"Hey, guys!"

The guest room was empty.

Chapter 5

☆

☆

A thousand possibilities ran through Sabrina's mind, none of them good. If only she could find Salem . . .

She ran for the stairs and was greeted with an amazing sight.

A teenage boy was chasing a black cat around the living room.

And a golden retriever was sitting up in an easy chair watching *Lassie* reruns on TV!

She started to call out to them, then stopped herself to look around. Where were her aunts? If she was lucky, they were ten million light-years away in the Other Realm. She tiptoed down the stairs to find out.

No such luck!

They were about ten *feet* away. Aunt Hilda was in her bathrobe, eating coffee cake and staring at the newspaper with sleepy-looking eyes. Aunt Zelda was in the dining room with her eyes glued to her notebook computer.

"Sabrina!" Salem hissed as he ran past her. "Do something!"

She did—she jumped in front of Macdougal as he came around. "Har-vey!" she said emphatically to remind him who he was supposed to be. "Maybe you should do your jogging *outside?*"

Dog-boy seemed to get the message and settled down.

"Have you had breakfast yet?" she asked him.

He shook his head and pointed toward the kitchen. "Sweet stuff, ugh! Got any Beef Stew? Liver Dinner? Prime Chunks in Gravy?"

Sabrina's stomach lurched at the names of what must be Macdougal's favorite canned dog food. Since all they had around the house was a finicky cat, their pet food supply was limited to tuna specialties and those dry little nibbly things. She could snap something up, but her aunts might be suspicious if they saw "Harvey" digging into a bowl of dog food for breakfast.

So she did the closest thing. She sat him down at the kitchen table with a bowl of canned beef stew— the kind humans like. It was almost the same thing.

Macdougal seemed to think so, too, but when Macdougal started to eat as if he were gobbling food from a dog bowl, she stuffed a huge mixing spoon in his hand. Along with a dishtowel for a bib, he seemed to do all right.

Aunt Hilda looked up from the paper. "No offense, Harvey, but how can you eat that stuff this early in the morning?"

But "Harvey" was too busy eating like a dog to answer.

"He's in training, Aunt Hilda," Sabrina quickly explained. "He's trying to bulk up for sports."

Hilda sighed. "I can't imagine what it's like having someone tell you to *gain* weight."

Sabrina began to relax a little. Apparently Aunt Hilda was too sleepy or too absorbed in her horoscope to notice anything weird about "Harvey."

But then, she had to admit, to the casual observer the difference between the real Harvey and the Harvey inhabited by the spirit of Macdougal the dog was slight.

Harvey usually didn't talk much, especially around adults.

Sabrina went into the dining room to scope out her other aunt. But Aunt Zelda was absorbed in writing some scientific paper. "By the way, Sabrina," she said as she stopped to save her most recent additions to her document. "I'm probably going to go work on my paper in the library. If you need something, just call me on my cell phone, all right?"

"Fine."

"I'll be leaving as soon as you and Harvey go to school."

"School?" Sabrina croaked.

Aunt Zelda looked over the top of her reading

glasses. "Wednesday is a traditional school day, last time I looked. Don't tell me there's another one of those teacher workdays?"

School? Yikes!

"Uh, no, there's school," Sabrina said brightly. "In fact, we can't wait to get there."

She hurried back into the living room and switched off the TV. Harvey the dog whimpered in disappointment.

"Um, Harvey—and Macdougal—and Salem, could I see you upstairs a minute?" She glanced at Hilda, who was still yawning over her second cup of coffee. "I think I'll keep Macdougal upstairs in my room while we're at school. Just so he doesn't run all over the house."

Hilda nodded sleepily. "Or we could zap him a fence out in the back—"

"Aunt Hilda?" Sabrina interrupted, giving her aunt the eye.

Hilda got the drift and smiled at Harvey. "What I mean to say is, too bad we don't have a fenced-in backyard. Then Macdougal could *zip* around out there all day."

"It's okay," Sabrina insisted. "Macdougal is used to being in the house during the day while his owners work. Right, Macdougal?"

"Right," both Macdougal and Harvey answered.

Sabrina nearly choked, and hoped the sound at least partway camouflaged the fact that two voices answered. But Hilda was now clipping a "Dear

Abby" column out of the paper and didn't seem to notice.

Thank goodness for small miracles, Sabrina thought, and led the gang upstairs.

"Okay, here's the plan," Sabrina said as they gathered in her room. "I thought about calling in sick for me and Harvey, but I don't know how I'd explain to everyone. Plus, we've got a big test today. And Harvey would just have to explain to his parents.

"So I've decided to take Macdougal to school and try to pass him off. Harvey, you usually don't talk much in class, so if we're lucky, I think we'll make it. And since we're in a lot of classes together, I'll keep an eye on him."

Harvey the dog jumped up onto Sabrina's bed, wound himself in a nice circle, then curled up for a nap. "School holiday—I can get into this. Besides, I didn't study much for the math test anyway. Maybe Macdougal will make a better grade than I would," he joked.

"Fine, now, Salem—" She stopped herself. "Come here, cat." She carried him to the small bay window with its stained-glass windowpanes and sat down with him. "Salem," she whispered, "you've got to promise to stay here and keep an eye on Harvey. Don't let him go anywhere without you."

Salem was still looking a little ruffled from being chased around downstairs. "It's like some horrible nightmare," he moaned.

"Oh, it's not that bad," Sabrina said. "And besides, I'm taking the real dog away. Harvey's not likely to chase you." She thought a moment. "Unless, of course, some of the natural dog instincts—"

"You'd better get to work on this fast," Salem meowed. "Because I don't think this arrangement is going to last."

Chapter 6

☆

"Macdougal! Stay!" Sabrina whispered angrily as she opened her locker inside the redbrick fortress known as Westbridge High School.

The dog who looked like Harvey leaned up against the lockers, panting softly with his tongue hanging out one side of his mouth. They had walked to school—actually, had run was more like it—and Macdougal had chased every cat, squirrel, bird, and U.S. Postal Service truck that they'd seen on the way.

Sabrina stuffed her books in her locker and took out the ones she needed for her first few classes. Then she slipped her arm through Harvey's—that is, the one Macdougal was temporarily borrowing!—and walked the dog to Harvey's locker. As she helped him with his books, she noticed Lloyd Krumley opening his locker nearby.

"Stop it!" he snapped when Sabrina glanced his way.

"What?"

"Don't look at my combination!" He wrapped his hand around his combination lock so she couldn't see which way he turned the dial.

"Good grief, Lloyd," she responded. "I'm not trying to figure out your combination." Why in the world would she possibly want to break into Lloyd Krumley's locker? She had a feeling that whatever he kept in there, she didn't want to see it.

Lloyd pushed his black plastic glasses up on his nose, pulled out his books, then slammed his locker closed and spun the lock. Suddenly he got a strange look on his face—a sort of surprised expression—and then—

"Ah-choo!" Frantically he reached into his shirt pocket for his individual packet of tissues and pulled one out. After blowing his nose—in an amazing imitation of a Canada goose's mating call—he looked around suspiciously. But before he could say anything, he erupted into a sneezing frenzy.

"Hey, Lloyd," Sabrina asked politely. "Are you all right?"

"Leave me alone!" Lloyd snapped, shouldering his backpack and stuffing a wad of tissues around his nose. "Somebody's up to something. And I'm going to tell." He stomped off.

"What was that all about?" Sabrina muttered.

But of course, Macdougal didn't have an opinion. He was too busy sniffing people's lockers.

"What are you doing?" Sabrina whispered, trying to drag him away. "People are staring!"

"Baloney!" Macdougal the boy barked friskily. "Smells good! Get some!" He started yanking on one of the lockers, trying to get inside.

"Macdougal! Stop that!" Sabrina ordered, pulling on his arm.

"Uh, excuse me . . ." Valerie walked hesitantly toward her two friends. "Uh, 'scuse me, Harvey. I hate to bother you and all, but—do you need something out of my locker?"

"Food!" Harvey growled, rattling the lock.

Valerie was new this year, but she'd gotten to know Harvey pretty well. In fact, occasionally the three of them wound up at the Slicery playing Foosball or just hanging out.

Sabrina panicked. Surely Valerie would know something was up with Harvey.

"His parents are out of town," Sabrina explained quickly. "Didn't get that home-cooked breakfast of champions this morning."

"Oh." Valerie opened her locker and started to put her things inside, including a bulging brown paper bag.

Suddenly Harvey's nose quivered as the dog inside him caught a whiff of Valerie's lunch. The aroma was so exhilarating to him, he nearly pointed. "Whatcha got?" he growled.

"Me?" Valerie peeked inside the bag and held up a thick sandwich wrapped in waxed paper. "Corned beef on rye." She studied Harvey's obvious expression of desire. "Would you like a—"

Chomp!

Macdougal attacked the sandwich and swallowed it in two bites. With a snort he spit out most of the waxed paper.

Valerie just stood there, her big brown eyes even wider, staring at her upheld fingers as if checking to make sure they were all still there. "—a bite?" she finished with a gulp.

"Guys are such animals when they're hungry," Sabrina commiserated. "Say thank you, Harvey."

"Thank you Harvey," Macdougal repeated obediently. *"Burrrrrp!"*

"Uh-huh. Glad you liked it, Harvey," Valerie said, her face pale against her long dark hair. "I, uh, guess I can buy lunch in the cafeteria today." Then she whispered to Sabrina, "Got any spare change? I'm broke."

Sabrina dug in her bag and handed her friend a five-dollar bill. "Take it. It's on me," she insisted. After all, she felt responsible for Macdougal's attack on her lunch.

Valerie shook her head. "No, I couldn't. I'll pay you back tomorrow—"

"Don't worry," Sabrina said through gritted teeth as she pulled Macdougal away. "Harvey *owes* me!"

* * *

Harvey's first class of the morning was chemistry, which was lucky, since Sabrina was also in that class. It was lucky, too, that they both sat near the back of the room. Sabrina hoped that would make it easy for her to keep Macdougal on a tight leash—so to speak.

As soon as they sat down, Donovan Stein turned around and gave them the good news: "We've got a sub for the rest of the week!"

"Excellent!" Sabrina gushed. Having a teacher who didn't know Harvey would make at least this class easier to get through.

Everyone whispered as a tiny woman with wild white hair entered the room and began to scrawl her name on the blackboard with trembling hands and a piece of squeaky chalk.

"Mrs. Dn-mrr-dl?" someone said doubtfully, squinting at the handwriting.

"That's Dubrovet," the teacher corrected.

Sabrina thought the woman looked like Albert Einstein's grandmother. Fortunately she didn't call on anyone, since she didn't know anybody's name. She seemed content to drone on and on in her soft high voice about the thrilling properties of each of her little "babies"—the various elements on the periodic table.

Macdougal put his head down on his desk between his paws (er, hands) and took a nap, along with about a third of the class.

So far so good, Sabrina thought. Maybe this *is* going to be pretty easy after all.

She sat back and began to enjoy the class. When she actually listened to the woman, she discovered that Mrs. Dubrovet was quite smart and had an enthusiasm for her subject that was quite unusual for a teacher at Westbridge High.

Besides, chemistry intrigued Sabrina. Perhaps she'd inherited some of the family genes that made Aunt Zelda such a whiz at science. Perhaps it had more to do with her experiences since she'd become a witch. The similarities between chemistry and magic were fascinating: both involved mixing separate elements together to create new—and often explosive—results. Time and again she found that the information in her chemistry book actually corresponded to things she was studying in her Witch's Handbook. Too bad she couldn't turn in any of her witch's homework for extra credit!

The class period went by quickly. Macdougal slept like a rock through the whole thing. When Westbridge High's annoyingly loud bell rang, the startled pooch jumped to his feet and barked.

Sabrina almost freaked, until she realized that the kids around him were laughing. They thought "Harvey" was just goofing off for the sub.

Apparently, typical high school male behavior was going to work in her favor.

"Come on, Macdougal," she whispered as she slipped an arm through his and led him into the crowded hallway. "You're doing great."

It was unnerving to see "Harvey" smile back with his usual sweet, crooked grin—the one that had captured her heart when she'd first come to Westbridge—and realize that it was actually a sweet, lovable dog responding to her praise.

But Macdougal continued to stare at her.

"What?" She glanced around to see if her shirt had come unbuttoned. "Have I got breakfast on my face or something?"

Macdougal whimpered as Harvey's face crumpled in disappointment.

Suddenly Sabrina got the point.

Apparently "praise" equaled "doggy treat" in the Milligen household.

She glanced around. Most kids were busy either sleepwalking, gossiping, or staring entranced into the eyes of their significant other. She didn't think anyone would notice a brief bit of witchery. With a quick blink, she zapped three small doggy cookies into her fist.

"Okay," she whispered as she slipped the reward into Harvey's hand. "But don't let anybody see what you're eating, okay?"

She needn't have worried. The treats disappeared instantly, as if they'd been inhaled.

"Thanks," Macdougal said with Harvey's lopsided grin.

Uh-oh! her internal radar screamed. *Incoming dog lick!*

Sabrina held out her hand and stopped him just in time. "Sorry, Macdougal, no offense," she whispered, "but licking girls on the face is not really an 'in' thing at Westbridge High."

"Really?"

"Trust me," she said.

Grabbing his arm, Sabrina maneuvered them through the mob and made it to English class seconds before the bell rang.

As they slid into their seats, Sabrina leaned forward and whispered, "Sit, Macdougal. Good dog. Stay."

Macdougal obeyed and sat still, happily looking around the room with that sweet dopey look of a dog who has absolutely nothing on his mind.

Sabrina chuckled. He should blend right in with most of the other students at Westbridge High.

But just at that moment one face stood out in the crowd—the annoying face of Libby Chessler. From her seat at the head of the class, the head cheerleader stared back at Sabrina and Harvey with narrowed eyes.

What was her problem? Surely she hadn't overheard Sabrina talking to Harvey like a dog—had she?

Sabrina shot her a fake grin—which worked like bug repellent. Libby whirled around in her seat and faced front.

"Okay, class, settle down," Mrs. Reilly said. She checked the roll, then handed back their latest book reports.

"Very good, Harvey," the teacher said as she stopped by his desk. She laid a paper with a big red B-plus at the top on his desk. "I found your paper discussing the similarities between Ernest Hemingway and Michael Jordan very thought-provoking. However, your spelling and grammar could use some improvement."

Luckily the teacher walked on. So she didn't see Harvey stick the paper in his mouth and rip off a bite.

"Harvey!" Sabrina hissed. "I mean—Macdougal! No!"

"No?"

"We don't tear up paper with our mouths," she whispered.

"Rrrrr," he grumbled. "But I like to."

"Okay," Sabrina whispered as she gently removed the paper from his hand. "But in private, when you get home, okay? Not at school."

"Okay," he said sadly. He sighed and tucked his head into his folded arms on his desk.

Sabrina's heart twisted. Poor Macdougal. She knew all this had to be tough on the poor pooch. How long till he gave in to his natural instincts and ran off? *Maybe I need to come up with something different to make this work,* she thought. *Or maybe . . .*

Suddenly Macdougal sat up in his chair with his ears pricked forward. He seemed enraptured by the teacher, as if she were a bird or squirrel he was stalking.

Oh, heavens, now what? Sabrina thought frantically. Did Mrs. Reilly remind him of the mailman?

Did her perfume smell like kielbasa? Had she accidentally sent out some centuries-old signal that dogs interpreted to mean "Chase me"?

But then Sabrina realized that the dog wasn't about to take Harvey's body and make a fool of it by dashing to the front of the classroom. He was actually frozen to his seat. Completely immobile. Could he be . . .

Listening?

Sabrina leaned out of her chair to take a better look. Sure enough, Dog Boy was actually listening to what the teacher was reading:

"And through it all Buck staggered along at the head of the team as in a nightmare. He pulled when he could; when he could no longer pull, he fell down and remained down till blows from whip or club drove him to his feet again. All the stiffness and gloss had gone out of his beautiful furry coat. . . . His muscles had wasted away to knotty strings. . . . It was heartbreaking, only Buck's heart was unbreakable. . . ."

Sabrina gasped. She'd been so intent on worrying about Harvey that she hadn't paid any attention to the teacher. They were beginning work on a new author, and Mrs. Reilly was reading a passage to introduce the class to the unique style and power of his language.

Sabrina noticed the blackboard for the first time and saw the title of the book the teacher was reading from.

The Call of the Wild, by Jack London. Written in 1903.

Sabrina had read this story once before. Her father had sent it to her three summers ago when she'd gone to summer camp. He'd met the author while in Alaska about a century ago, he'd written. It was a wonderful book and she just *had* to read it.

The story was told through the eyes of the dog Buck, who was stolen from his comfortable middle-class home and forced to work as a sled dog during the Alaskan gold rush. As he was passed from owner to owner, Buck was mistreated by man and dog alike.

In the scene Mrs. Reilly was reading, Buck's inexperienced new owner had overloaded the dog-sled and was beating the dogs, trying to make them get up and go. Starving and exhausted, Buck refused to get up. And still the blows continued to fall.

Mrs. Reilly placed a finger in her book to hold her place. "When you read an author's work aloud, something magical happens. It helps you hear the special music of that particular writer's voice. It helps you experience his talent for storytelling. You can almost imagine you actually hear the writer in your head."

Mrs. Reilly smiled. "I think I'd like one of you to

take over and read the next paragraph or two—to see what I mean." She scanned the room, looking for a face to call on.

Instantly kids ducked behind others and held their breath. In the silence that followed, a small sound could be heard.

A soft whimper.

Sabrina patted Harvey's shoulder. "Macdougal—shhh!"

And then Mrs. Reilly looked their way.

Yikes! She's going to call on me, Sabrina thought frantically. *No, please, Mrs. Reilly,* she begged in her mind. *Not today. I'm too busy dog-sitting!*

But the teacher's eyes didn't land on Sabrina.

Then that meant—

No! She couldn't—

Sabrina's heart thundered like horse's hooves.

"Harvey," Mrs. Reilly said. "Would you stand up, please?"

Chapter 7

Macdougal was a good dog. Too good a dog.

He stood up on command.

So now the entire class was staring at the teacher's victim, Harvey Kinkle. He looked as if he were about to cry. But only Sabrina knew that he was really a dog in boy's clothing.

"I couldn't help but notice how moved you seemed to be by Buck's sad story," Mrs. Reilly commented with a smile. She was obviously impressed by his sensitivity.

"Harvey" just nodded.

"Have you read *The Call of the Wild* before?"

"No—" Macdougal choked out.

"Oh." Mrs. Reilly walked down the aisle and placed the book in his hands. Then she showed him where to begin. "Will you read this for us, please?"

Harvey appeared to stare uncomprehendingly at the pages before him. "I—I can't," Macdougal blurted out.

You're barking up the wrong tree with this one, Sabrina thought as she sank down in her seat. Macdougal had just told the entire class that Harvey Kinkle couldn't read. How long would that take to get around school? She had the feeling she was going to need some magic—and fast.

Mrs. Reilly's hand flew to her chest. A single tear escaped from the corner of her eye and trickled down her cheek as she gazed at her student.

She didn't think that Harvey couldn't read because he didn't know how.

She thought Harvey couldn't read because he was too choked up over the story!

Mrs. Reilly patted Harvey's arm and whispered, "I understand." She took the book from his hands and quietly made her way back to the front of the classroom. "Don't worry, Harvey," she said kindly. "Listen to what happens next." She began to read once more:

"And then, suddenly, without warning, uttering a cry that was inarticulate and more like the cry of an animal, John Thornton sprang upon the man who wielded the club. . . ."

Mrs. Reilly's eyes shone as she read the familiar words.

"John Thornton stood over Buck, struggling to control himself, too convulsed with rage to speak.

'If you strike that dog again, I'll kill you. . . .'"

If Harvey had had a tail, Macdougal would have been wagging it.

Smiling, Sabrina grabbed him by the sleeve and gently tugged him back into his seat.

Whaddya know, she chuckled to herself. A dog with a taste for great literature. The real Harvey had better prepare himself when he came back to school.

It looked like Macdougal had just gotten him promoted to teacher's pet.

Somehow Sabrina managed to get Harvey through all his morning classes without revealing his secret identity.

But at lunchtime, it took all her strength to get Macdougal through the lunch line without him crawling headfirst into the huge metal pans of steaming-hot food. He was probably the first kid ever in the history of high school to look excited about the oddly shaped mystery meat covered with lumpy gray goo the lunch-line ladies affectionately referred to as their "secret-recipe gravy."

One of the servers—a tiny birdlike woman with thick glasses perched on a long nose—cackled with glee when Sabrina bought him three full lunches. "I like a young man with a good appetite!" she said, tugging at her hairnet. She leaned forward and gave him a wink. "How about a little extra gravy, sonny?"

"Woof!" Macdougal answered, drooling onto the front of his plaid flannel shirt.

The old lady giggled. "What a character!" she exclaimed, and gave him an extra biscuit.

Rolling her eyes, Sabrina dragged Macdougal past her regular table in search of a table that was not so public. At last she found one so far off in a corner that even the nerds ignored it.

If they were lucky, no one would notice them.

If they were lucky, no one would see "Harvey" eating like a *dog!*

But, of course, Valerie found them. After all, she was the editor of the *Westbridge Lantern,* and she was pretty good at sniffing out news.

Sabrina wondered if Valerie would notice how different Harvey was, but she was busy chattering away about her latest article for the newspaper. And Harvey was busy scarfing down his mystery meat with extra gravy and biscuits, and his occasional grunts of pleasure only seemed like his usual brief comments.

But the stress of waiting for something to go wrong was wearing Sabrina out.

As soon as possible Sabrina mumbled some excuse and hustled Macdougal away from the table.

Maybe coming to school wasn't such a good idea

after all, she thought as they took their trays to the trash. If it weren't for that math test this afternoon . . .

Suddenly Harvey disappeared. But he'd been right there! Frantically Sabrina looked around—and then she spotted him.

At least the rear end of him.

"Macdougal!" She hissed. "Get your head out of the trash!"

Harvey looked as if he were being swallowed by one of the huge gray plastic lunchroom trash cans. Sabrina tried to block the view. She pulled on his belt to try to drag him out, but he was too strong. And too determined!

"Lose something?"

A chill ran up Sabrina's spine. But that was normal. The voice of Mr. Kraft, the vice-principal, usually struck terror in her heart no matter what she was up to.

"Macdougal!" she hissed under her breath. "Out of the trash—now!—or you sleep outside tonight."

Slowly she turned around, yanking Macdougal by his plaid flannel sleeve. A little piece of spinach clung to his cheek, and she quickly brushed it away.

Mr. Kraft peered through his wire-rimmed glasses at them as he clutched his tiny spiral-bound notebook and pencil to his chest, ready and waiting to record a student demerit. His usual expression made him look as if he'd just sucked a sour pickle. Right now it looked as if he'd swallowed three.

Quick, Sabrina! Think! . . . Of course!

"Retainer," she said simply.

"Really," Mr. Kraft drawled.

Sabrina nodded. "Left it on the lunch tray. Boom! Tossed it with the trash."

"Children!" Mr. Kraft exclaimed with a sigh. "You should be more careful. Your parents work hard to pay for these things. They don't deserve your irresponsible behavior."

"Yes, Mr. Kraft," Sabrina said submissively, hoping he'd just leave.

Mr. Kraft glared at "Harvey."

"He's sorry, too," Sabrina hastily added.

Mr. Kraft frowned. His scruffy white mustache twitched as if he smelled something fishy—and not just the cafeteria refuse. But then he spotted some students running in the hall, and with a stern look of warning, he finally walked away.

"Macdougal, let's—"

"Sabrina? *Sabrina!*"

Oh, great, Sabrina thought. She knew who that was. Who else would shout her name in a way that let everyone know exactly what she thought of Sabrina? *All I need now is Libby Chessler sticking her new nose into my business.*

"Oh, hi, Libby. Looking for some dessert?"

The head cheerleader glared at Sabrina. "Excuse me, but if it's any of your business—which it is *not*—I was trying to get past you to ask Harvey about our western civilization project." Then her brown eyes narrowed suspiciously. "By the way, why do you keep calling Harvey 'Macdougal'?"

Sabrina choked, then laughed. "What? Give me a break, Libby." She laughed some more as if Libby had told an outrageous joke.

Libby and Macdougal just stared at her.

Sabrina shrugged. "Why would I call him 'Macdougal'?"

Macdougal started to speak. "Because it's my na—"

Zap! Sabrina wiggled her pinky and wrapped an invisible muzzle around Macdougal's mouth.

"Mmmf!" Macdougal tried, then shrugged and gave up. It was a lot more fun watching a roach crawl up the wall beside the trash can anyway.

"That's exactly what I was wondering," Libby said. "It's a strange thing to do—even for a freak like you."

"But I—"

"Don't deny it," Libby warned, jamming her hands onto her hips. "I heard you—just now, and earlier today, in English, and another time in the hall."

Sabrina smiled confidently as inside she panicked, searching for an explanation.

"Well, it was supposed to be our little secret," Sabrina made up.

Libby's nose twitched. "Secret?" she asked eagerly.

"Yeah, it's kind of a pet name for him," Sabrina

said as she slipped her arm through his. "Kind of an in joke, you know. And he calls me . . ."

"Woof!" Macdougal managed to say through the invisible muzzle—in Harvey's voice, of course.

Libby raised one eyebrow.

"Wolf!" Sabrina repeated, inching toward Libby. "You know, like the large, sleek predatory animals that often *attack* when cornered?"

Libby jumped back a step, startled. Then she frowned in disgust, pulling her arms close around her as if she were afraid she'd be contaminated. "Sabrina Spellman, you are weird!"

She turned her attention to Harvey, a male—which instantly activated her internal eyelash-fluttering mechanism. "Harvey," she said sweetly. "I thought you and Sabrina weren't seeing each other anymore."

"We're just good friends," Sabrina interrupted. "I know it's a strange concept for you, Libby, but it's something some of us ordinary people do on a regular basis—make friends."

"How brave of you to admit you're ordinary," Libby countered. Then she turned her attention back to Harvey. "So why do you hang around with her? You're so much more—"

Libby froze as "Harvey" started to sniff her face.

"Ewww! Get off me!" she shrieked, stumbling backward. "Harvey Kinkle, you'd better stop hanging around with Sabrina Spellman. It's making you weird, too!" Spinning on the toe of her chunky black shoes, she marched off toward her usual flock of admirers, no doubt to gossip about Sabrina and Harvey.

"Come on, Mac," Sabrina muttered, walking the dog out of the cafeteria. "It's time for our math test."

She was halfway down the hall before she noticed she was by herself. "Macdougal!" she shouted sternly over her shoulder, finally losing patience. "Come!"

A dozen students around her stared as if she were crazy.

"Talk about possessive!" muttered some boy in the crowd.

Sabrina sighed and rubbed her aching temples. *Will this day ever end?*

Mrs. Quick gave them her usual cheery smile as they headed into class. Sabrina was doing great in math this year, and she hadn't been worried about the test—until now.

All Macdougal wanted to do was chew on his pencils, but Sabrina put a stop to that. She was worried he'd hurt Harvey's teeth.

Sabrina put her books under her desk, then stopped. What in the cosmos was Macdougal up to now?

He was squirming and twisting around in his seat, and it looked as if he were trying to get his foot up to his shoulder.

"Macdougal, you don't have to scratch like that now," she whispered.

"Rrrf?"

"Hands!" Sabrina hissed. "You've got hands now. It's way easier."

Macdougal held up Harvey's hands in front of his face. "Forgot." The itchy spot was quickly taken care of the human way.

At last Mrs. Quick began to pass out the test papers.

"Okay, Macdougal," Sabrina whispered. "When you get your test, don't do anything. Just pick up a pencil and hold on to it. I'll do all the rest."

Macdougal turned around and looked at her with a hopeful grin.

"Yeah, yeah, yeah," Sabrina agreed hurriedly. "Be good during the test, and I'll reward you with more doggie cookies."

"Arf!" Macdougal said, slapping her a high five.

Sabrina stared. "Where'd you learn to do *that?*"

"Harvey taught me," Macdougal answered. Then he sighed. "I miss Harvey."

"Don't worry, you'll see him tonight," Sabrina assured him. "I promise. Now, be a good doggie and take your test."

"No talking," Mrs. Quick said in that sweet but firm voice she had.

Sabrina quickly quieted down. She had to be careful. The last thing she needed was for Mrs. Quick to pay her extra attention while she was conducting one of the weirdest experiments in the history of mathematics.

When Sabrina got her test, she quickly scanned the problems. Good, not too tough.

She winked at Macdougal, then cast a spell:

*"When my fingers write a number
Your little fingers will write the same.
All my answers will be your answers,
But on your paper you'll write Harvey's name."*

Mrs. Quick cleared her throat. "Sabrina? Do you have something you'd like to say to the class?"

"Uh, no, Mrs. Quick," Sabrina answered with an embarrassed smile, then blurted out, "It's just this little, um, good-luck thing I always say before a test. You know—silly superstition."

Libby and her friend Cee Cee snorted with laughter.

How would you like to spend the rest of your life as a protractor? Sabrina longed to say. Only Aunt Zelda's lectures about self-restraint enabled Sabrina to keep her twitching finger curled up inside her balled-up fists.

"All right, then," Mrs. Quick said. "But perhaps you should get started now."

Sabrina ducked her head over her paper. *Okay, let's see if this works.*

Sabrina read through problem one. Then, as her pencil began to make marks on her paper, Macdougal jumped. Holding on to his pencil, he watched in fascination as his hand began to move on the page—actually writing numbers! Whatever Sabrina wrote, Macdougal had to write. He held the pencil awkwardly, and the numbers came out a little wobbly. But then, that was pretty much the way the real Harvey wrote anyway.

The whole test would have been a lot easier to take if Lloyd Krumley hadn't been sitting right in front of Macdougal. He sniffled and sneezed through the entire test.

One by one Sabrina made her way through the problems on the quiz.

One by one Macdougal's hands wrote down the same answers.

When they were finished, Sabrina undid the spell.

"One by one, and two by two,
The power in your fingers returns to you."

But then, on second thought, she fluttered her fingertips back and forth to get Macdougal to erase a couple of answers. If Harvey suddenly got an excellent score on a math test, Mrs. Quick would be suspicious—especially if Harvey and Sabrina's test papers matched exactly.

Near the end of the class Mr. Kraft came on the intercom.

"Attention. Attention, please. This is Mr. Kraft, your vice-principal, with an important announcement. It has come to my attention that someone is hiding an animal at school."

What? Sabrina thought. She glanced worriedly at Harvey. *How in the world did he—*

Her eyes fell on Lloyd Krumley. He was nodding self-righteously, so hard his glasses kept sliding down his nose. *Why, that whiny little rat!*

He's allergic to Macdougal.

"Such infractions of school discipline and public health will not be tolerated," Mr. Kraft went on. "No dogs are allowed on school property. And that means hallways, classrooms, entryways, rest rooms, grounds, and sports fields. I repeat, no dogs are allowed on school property. Period. I demand that the student with the animal come clean and report to my office immediately."

Lloyd Krumley was so caught up in Mr. Kraft's speech that when the principal finished, he began to whistle and clap. When he realized he was the only one applauding, he slunk down into his chair and blew his nose.

Mr. Kraft was not through. "So turn yourself in," he repeated, "or I will personally track you down like the dog you are and suspend you from school. Do I make myself clear?"

"Woof!" Macdougal said.

Several kids in the class snickered.

"Thank you," Mr. Kraft said. "And have a nice—never mind."

Oh, great! Sabrina thought as she tried to stop Harvey—doggone it! Macdougal!—from licking up a spill on the floor. *We're in the doghouse now!*

☆

Chapter 8

☆

Finally the final bell rang and Sabrina led Macdougal to Harvey's locker.

"Walk," Macdougal grunted.

Sabrina frowned. "Look, Macdougal, I'm in a hurry. You're a very nice dog, but this day has worn me out. Let's just get our things and go home, okay?"

"Walk," he repeated.

"All right, all right, I'll slow down."

"Walk!"

"I *am* walking!"

"No," Macdougal snarled, "I need a walk. Out-side."

"But—" Sabrina stopped and looked him in the eye. "You mean like . . ."

Macdougal nodded.

Good grief! That was something she'd totally forgotten to plan for.

"Listen, Macdougal," she whispered. "People don't go outside for that kind of walk. You must have noticed."

Macdougal shrugged and shuffled Harvey's feet. "Gotta go!" he insisted.

Sabrina groaned. This was very uncomfortable, but a girl had to do what a girl had to do. She stood on tiptoe and whispered into Harvey's ear, explaining the way things were to the confused Macdougal.

Harvey's eyes popped open in surprise, and then he shrugged. "Okay. Show me where."

Blushing to the roots of her blond hair, Sabrina showed him where the boys' room was, shooed him in, and waited outside.

And waited, and waited. Time sure went slow when you were waiting for a dog to figure out how to be a human.

Finally she couldn't stand it. She looked around. The halls were clearing out quite a bit, and no one seemed to be coming this way. So she opened the boys' room door and stuck her head in, careful, of course, to keep her eyes shut tight. "Macdou—I mean, Harvey!" she hissed, in case any other guys were in there. "What are you doing in there? Are you okay?"

Just then Jason Wayne, a senior on the track team, came up behind her. "Hey, Sabrina," he teased, "the girls' room is that way."

Feeling her blush deepen into a new shade of scarlet, Sabrina stepped aside to let Jason pass. "Uh, 'scuse me, Jason," she said. "But, um, Harvey went in there a long time ago. I'm worried he might be sick or something. Can you sort of check on him, make sure he's okay?"

"Sure thing, Sabrina."

He pushed open the door and strolled inside. "Hey, Kinkle!" he shouted at the top of his lungs. "Your lady's waiting for you!"

If my face gets any hotter, Sabrina thought with clenched teeth, *I won't need a stove to boil water for hot chocolate.*

A few minutes later "Harvey" strolled out with his buddy Jason, who was explaining a play from last night's major-league baseball game on TV. Harvey seemed to be nodding. Surely Macdougal didn't understand baseball!

But then Sabrina realized that Macdougal was simply bobbing his head up and down as he watched a fly buzzing around his head.

"Okay, buddy," Jason said at last, "catch you at track practice."

Track practice! Sabrina thought. *No way am I taking Macdougal to track practice. Sorry, Coach. Harvey's skipping practice today.*

"Hey, don't forget, man," Jason reminded Harvey. "Coach Tripp said if we miss practice this week, we're off the team. We got a lot of work to do if we're even going to place at the meet this weekend."

Great, Sabrina thought. *If I take Macdougal home now, Harvey will get kicked off the team. But Harvey loves track. He'd never forgive me!*

Jason waved good-bye, then turned to go—

Just as "Harvey" snapped at—and caught—the enticing fly. In his *mouth!*

Ewwwwww! Sabrina nearly barfed. She looked at that face, the face of Harvey Kinkle that she'd known and loved.

That does it! she thought as her blush began to turn a weird shade of green. *Now I know Harvey and I will never get back together—'cause I could never, ever kiss that fly-chomping mouth again! Yuck!*

Somehow she got Macdougal to track practice, dressed in a quickly zapped duplicate of Harvey's track suit.

Coach Tripp was already giving his team a pep talk. "All right, all right, so the captain of the Ridgefield team called the Fighting Scallions a bunch of veggie burgers. So what? Veggie burgers are low in fat—and so are we!"

Whoa, some logic, Sabrina thought with a laugh. But she had to admire the coach's optimism in the face of impending doom. The track team had a pretty poky reputation.

All the Westbridge teams were supposed to be the Fighting Stallions. But a typo at the printer had forever sealed their fate as fighting vegetables instead of fighting horses. Sabrina thought that maybe if the athletes all *ate* scallions before each sporting event—and grossed out their opponents with onion breath—they might have a better record.

She whispered some instructions to Macdougal about what to do at practice and reminded him to be on his best behavior. Then she took a seat on the bleachers, where she could see everything. If things got out of hand, she'd just have to surreptitiously use her magic to keep Macdougal—and Harvey—out of hot water.

A few minutes later, as she watched the team warm up, her friend Valerie plopped down beside her in the bleachers and dropped her bulging backpack to the cement floor.

"What are you doing here?" Sabrina asked, surprised.

"I'm covering the track meet for the school paper."

"But you're the editor, not the sports reporter," Sabrina pointed out. "And the meet's not till Saturday."

"Yeah, but the paper's coming out Friday morning and we're doing a cover story to encourage kids to come to the meet on Saturday." She grinned sheepishly. "And I pulled rank to cover the story. It may be wishful thinking"—her voice dropped to a whisper—"but I keep hoping that if I do good stories on all these cute athletes, one of them will ask me out."

Sabrina smiled and gave her friend a quick hug. "Don't worry, Valerie. You're a diamond in the rough. The right guy's gonna come along and find you one of these days."

"I guess so," Valerie said wistfully. "I just hope by then that I'll still be young enough to enjoy it."

Sabrina's laughter was cut short when she saw a blur rocket down the track.

A blur that looked a lot like Harvey Kinkle!

"Did you see that?" Sabrina exclaimed.

A stunned Valerie nodded. "Who was that?" And then she quickly grabbed her reporter's notebook and started scribbling down some notes.

Down below, Harvey's teammates were hollering and cheering as they watched him race around the track. But then the cheering turned into puzzled chatter when "Harvey" veered off the track at the other end and kept going!

Uh-oh. "Um, excuse me, Valerie," Sabrina said quickly, "I'll be right back."

Valerie was busy writing, so she just waved without looking up.

Sabrina dashed down to the back of the bleachers. She checked to see if anybody was watching, but everyone's eyes seemed glued to Harvey's mysterious run.

First she stopped time for the people at the track (*Book of Magic*, page 201). The track team froze as if she'd hit the Pause button on a VCR.

Then she attempted a molecular transference.

Her aunts and other supernatural relatives did it all the time. So did the Quizmaster. But it was new magic for her—a girl who'd spent sixteen years traveling in the mortal realm—and it was one of the trickier tricks she'd learned so far from the Witch's Handbook.

She was standing behind the bleachers.

She concentrated on the magic.

And a millisecond later—*bing!*—she appeared next to Macdougal in the runaway Harvey body. "Macdougal!" she exclaimed. "What in the world happened—"

"Do you want sauerkraut with that?" a hot-dog vendor was saying as he held up three steaming dogs. Apparently he'd missed seeing her appear out of thin air.

Sabrina watched his sales technique. No wonder. The guy was so bored with his job, he was totally oblivious.

Without blinking an eyelash, Macdougal wolfed down the dogs, buns and all.

"Hey!" the man cried, wiping his hands on his grimy white apron. "You gotta pay for them dogs first!"

"Don't worry." Sabrina pulled some bills from her pocket. "Will this cover it?"

The man nodded and took the bills.

"Come on, Macdougal," Sabrina said, taking his hand to lead him back to the track meet.

And then he did something funny.

He licked her hand.

Sabrina thought it felt pretty weird, but she had to laugh. *I guess that's "dog talk" for "thanks,"* she thought.

She smiled into Harvey's shining brown eyes and realized that she saw there, for the first time, not Harvey, but the soul of Macdougal, who'd enjoyed the exhilarating freedom of an unleashed run. He was a good-natured dog who was actually coping pretty well for being a human for the first time—especially a human in high school.

"Hey, fella," Sabrina said softly. "You're doing okay. I'm proud of you."

"Arf!" he replied, borrowing Harvey's famous lopsided grin.

"And I promise you, when we get home, I'm going to figure out how to switch you and Harvey back."

Macdougal shrugged. "It's okay. Being people is kinda fun."

When they got back to the track, Sabrina undid the stop-time spell, and instantly Harvey's teammates crowded around him, raving about his run.

"Harvey, my man, your running has majorly improved," Jason told him, slapping him on the back.

"You run like a greyhound!" the coach gushed.

Macdougal's eyes lit up. "Thanks!"

Everyone started talking at once about the meet on Saturday. Harvey's dashing dash seemed to have sent a bolt of electricity through the entire team. Instead of assuming they were going to get creamed, the guys were now talking about how far they could go.

Back in the bleachers, Sabrina found her best friend working on her front-page story. "I know I don't have a chance of going out with Harvey," Valerie said, then quickly added for Sabrina's benefit, "And of course I never would even if he asked me. But I'm going to write about him anyway. Did you see him run? We might even have a shot at the regional track meet this weekend."

Sabrina grinned. "You might be right."

The rest of the practice was amazing. It was almost as if the athletes had been sleeping, and now they'd awakened refreshed and raring to go. They seemed like a whole new team.

And then something *really* weird happened—Sabrina found herself actually getting excited about *track.* And who knew? Maybe the team would do well on Saturday. After all, attitude and inspiration could work some pretty powerful magic.

The only time Sabrina had to interfere was when Macdougal started chasing a squirrel.

But Harvey's teammates didn't question their star runner. They just followed his crazy zigzag run around the field, figuring it was a new training technique.

Hmm, Sabrina thought. *Maybe, with a sprinkle of magic, we can make this work for us.*

She turned her head and whispered, so Valerie wouldn't hear:

> *"Furry gray squirrel*
> *With the question-mark tail,*
> *Run circles round the track*
> *To keep Mac on your trail."*

The squirrel began to circle the black cinder track, and Macdougal chased the swift-footed little creature at breakneck speed.

Harvey's teammates followed without question.

The coach checked his stopwatch and shook his head in amazement. "That kid might even break a record this weekend!" he shouted.

"Whoo-hoo!" Sabrina yelled as she and Valerie stood up and cheered.

You can thank me later, Harvey, she thought with a satisfied smile.

By the end of practice, though, Sabrina was exhausted, even though she wasn't even on the team. She was glad they could finally go home.

"You were great out there today, Macdougal," Sabrina said as they walked home.

"Wait'll I tell Harvey," Macdougal gushed. "Track is so cool!"

"You're a natural," Sabrina agreed.

Harvey threw back his head, threw out his arms, and shouted to the sky, "I love being a boy!"

A lady on the sidewalk jumped nearly two feet.

With a worried frown, she grabbed her two children by the hand and hurried away.

About a block from school, Macdougal stopped suddenly and raised his leg toward a fire hydrant.

"Macdougal!" Sabrina shrieked.

Dog-boy just laughed. "Chill," he said as he propped his sneakered foot on the hydrant. "Gotta tie my shoe." And then he quickly executed a perfect bow.

Sabrina was amazed. "Hey, you're a dog. How'd you learn how to do that?"

"Arf," Macdougal woofed. "Easy. Dogs have paws and a nose. With fingers, everything's a piece of cake!"

Sabrina laughed. "Come on, Wonder Boy. Let's go home."

It had been a tough day, but they'd made it through okay. And Sabrina had to admit it had also been kind of fun. After all, how many people got to spend the day talking—really talking—to a dog? It had definitely been an experience to remember.

Still, it would be nice to get Harvey and Macdougal back to normal, too.

But when she shoved open the huge wooden front door of her aunts' Victorian home, she discovered Salem sitting on the stairs, waiting for her. By the look of his fur and the sharp flick of his tail, she knew he was as mad as a cat on a hot tin roof.

"Salem!" she exclaimed, afraid to ask what she knew she must. "What's wrong?"

"It's Macdougal—I mean Harvey—oh! whoever he is—that *dog!*" he yowled.

Oh, no! Harvey? "Where is he?" Sabrina demanded. "Is he all right? What happened?"

Salem's eyes narrowed to tiny slits. "He decided to go for a little walk," he told her.

"Didn't you go with him?"

"I tried," Salem insisted. "But he went nuts when he got out—he was running too fast. And then"—Salem winced—"he got picked up by the dogcatcher!"

Sabrina screamed.

But Macdougal laid a reassuring paw, or hand, on Sabrina's arm. "Tags," he said simply.

"Tags?" And then Sabrina sighed in relief. "Of course. Macdougal's right. Harvey was wearing dog tags—Macdougal's tags. He'll be all right. They'll bring him back or call us."

"Uh-uh," Macdougal said.

Sabrina frowned. "What do you mean?"

"Milligens. Tags have the *Milligens'* number."

"Oh, yeah." Sabrina ran her hand through her hair, thinking. "Do they have an answering machine? Do you have a key to their house? Maybe we could—"

"Never mind," Salem interrupted.

"What do you mean, never mind?" Sabrina said, shocked.

"He's not, um, wearing them," Salem explained. "His tags."

"But—"

"Now, don't get mad at *me*"—Salem backed up toward the stairs—"but—"

"Salem!" Sabrina shrieked angrily. "What did you do?"

"Nothing! Harvey took his collar off!"

"What?" Sabrina exclaimed. "But why? And how? Tell me, Salem Saberhagen—how can a dog take off his own collar?"

"I don't know exactly," Salem said defensively. "But he said he wasn't used to it. He said it was worse than a tie and he just had to take it off."

"I don't believe you."

"It's true!" Salem put his little black paw on his chest. "Cross my heart. Remember, Sabrina, he's not a dog. Well, he is and he isn't. It's like me. He has—how shall we say?—some physical limitations based on his current biological manifestation. But inside, where it matters, he's still a very human Harvey. And Harvey's a lot smarter than any dumb dog."

Macdougal growled.

"Heel," Sabrina said absently as she sat down on the steps next to Salem to think. Macdougal grumbled, but lay down on the floor against the front door.

"You know that full-length mirror in your room?" Salem asked. "Harvey looked into that so he could see the collar. Did you ever think of doing that, bone breath?" Salem asked Macdougal.

Macdougal frowned. "What's a mirror?"

"Never mind!" Salem took a deep breath. "Anyway, somehow, using the nails on his paw, Harvey managed to pick at the buckle and get it undone. It took him forever."

Sabrina nodded. "Harvey may be slow sometimes, but he *is* persistent."

"Anyway," Salem went on. "Then he insisted he had to go for a walk. But when he got outside, he didn't."

"Didn't what?"

"Walk," Salem explained. "He ran. As in *away*."

"Salem!" Sabrina groaned. "How could you let him get away?"

"Excuse me?" Salem said. "Look, I'm the one shedding from the stress here. And on what planet is it," he added sarcastically, "where you think a *cat* is able to stop a *dog* from doing *anything*? Harvey *chose* to run around the neighborhood without proper canine identification."

"But that means—"

"Yep," Salem said in a tone of voice that clearly said he thought all dogs were ultimate boneheads. "They'll throw him in the pound like a common stray."

Chapter 9

☆

Without another word, Sabrina scooped up her black cat, grabbed Macdougal by his human arm, and molecularly transferred them all to a spot behind a huge yellow forsythia bush in bloom right outside the city pound.

"Whoa!" Macdougal said, rocking dizzily on Harvey's two legs. "Radical!"

"Macdougal," Sabrina whispered. "Where did you pick up all this slang?"

"Mrs. Milligen," he explained. "She cleans house to MTV."

"Now, listen, Macdougal," Sabrina said. "You be a good dog inside, all right? They may ask you a bunch of questions about Harvey the dog. But just let me do most of the talking, okay?"

"You go, girl!" he said, then chewed at an itch on his shoulder with his teeth.

"Sheesh!" Sabrina said as she led boy and cat inside.

She smiled at the woman at the front desk, who wore a tag that said, "Hi, I'm Marsha!"

"We're looking for a lost golden retriever," Sabrina explained. "Do you know if one has been brought in?"

"I just came on duty," Marsha said. "But I can take you back to look."

"Great!" She followed the woman back into the kennels.

Immediately all the dogs started barking like crazy—whether at Salem the cat or something about Macdougal, Sabrina wasn't sure. Macdougal, in Harvey's tall lean body, clung to one of the cages and barked back.

Marsha stared.

"Oh, don't mind him," Sabrina said, thinking quickly. "He's a method actor. And he's got this kids' theater thing coming up soon where he's supposed to be a dog."

"Oh, really? I'd *love* to see that!" Marsha said.

"I'll send you a flyer," Sabrina promised.

Salem dug his claws into her forearm. "Sabrina," he whispered, tickling her ear with his whiskers, "this is making me very nervous."

"Ouch! Relax. We'll be out of here in a second," she told him just as Marsha looked back at her.

The woman smiled knowingly. "I talk to my cat, too."

Frantically Sabrina searched for a dog that

looked like Macdougal. But there were so many cages, and so many animals. Sabrina couldn't believe so many pets could be lost, abandoned, or strays.

"Psst! Sabrina! Over here!"

"Did you say something, dear?" Marsha asked.

"Uh, no, ma'am," Sabrina said. "But I think I see our dog." They hurried down the cement floor to the last cage, where Harvey the dog pressed his black nose against the cage.

"We found him!" she called to Marsha.

Marsha came over and looked at the well-cared-for, purebred golden retriever—without his tag. "You really should put a collar and tag on your dog," she scolded.

"We did, only it came off," Sabrina explained quickly. "Can we have him now?"

"Do you have proof of ownership?" Marsha asked.

Uh-oh. "Like what?" Sabrina asked.

"Papers of some kind. This is a purebred golden," Marsha said. "He's valuable. We have to be sure he's yours."

"Well, he's not exactly ours," Sabrina explained. "My friend Harvey here"—she patted Macdougal on the back—"is dog-sitting for his next-door neighbors."

"Oh." Marsha looked them both over. "Really. Well, I have to be sure. I can't release one of our dogs to just anybody."

"Psst!"

Sabrina peeked at the dog in question.

"Wallet!" he whispered.

"Excuse me?" Marsha said.

"Wallet," Sabrina said. Then realized, "Wallet! Macdougal—I mean *Harvey*—look in your wallet!"

"Wallet?" Macdougal asked, puzzled. "What's a—"

"Here you go!" Sabrina dug in his back pants pocket, where she knew Harvey always carried his wallet. She opened it up, smiling at Marsha, as she wondered what exactly it was that she was looking for. *Hmmm, driver's license, thirteen bucks— awww, a picture of me!—a bent baseball card, a couple of stamps . . .*

Inside the cage Harvey barked impatiently.

Sabrina shot him a look that said, *You should have thought about that before you went joyriding with Macdougal's legs!*

And then she found it. A folded-up sheet of white paper. She read the words—"rabies vaccination record," the name "Macdougal" and a description of the dog, along with the name and address of Macdougal's veterinarian. The Milligens must have given it to Harvey just in case, or perhaps so he'd have their vet's phone number.

That satisfied Marsha. She seemed impressed by a young man who would carry a dog's vaccination record around in his wallet. She released the dog from its cage, and Sabrina reached into her shoulder bag and hunted up a collar and leash.

"I've got his collar and tags right here," she said. "Bad dog, don't do that again." She slipped them around the dog's neck. "Sorry, Harvey," she whispered, clipping on the leash.

"It's okay, Sab," he whispered back. "After this afternoon's adventure, I'm enjoying the security."

Back home at last, relieved to see her aunts weren't home, Sabrina hustled the gang up to her room.

Salem curled up in the late evening sunlight streaming in through the stained-glass window. "Wake me up," he said snippily, "when this is a dog-free zone again."

Harvey and Macdougal sat on Sabrina's bed.

"Okay," Sabrina began. "I have an idea about how to change you back."

"Tell us," Harvey said, wagging Macdougal's long feathery tail.

Sabrina laughed. The dog looked so cute with Harvey's voice coming out of his mouth. *What a great TV show we could make with this!*

"Well, it's complicated, and I'd probably better not tell you the details," Sabrina said. "I might get Aunt Zelda in trouble."

"We won't tell," Harvey said. "Will we, Macdougal?"

"Woof," Macdougal agreed.

Sabrina was actually going to start with a simple reversal spell—which was essentially like typing control-z on her aunt's computer, the command for

Undo. She had read last night that sometimes even a spell that seemed dramatic might actually have simple astral-biological properties that made it a snap to reverse.

But of course, she couldn't let Harvey know that she was using witchcraft to switch him back into his own body.

"Okay, guys, this is going to be a little messy, but hopefully, effective. Now, close your eyes . . ."

Boy and dog closed their eyes.

Sabrina muttered the words to the basic reversal spell under her breath. But to make it look good, she snapped her fingers to zap two test tubes of bubbling—but harmless—purple liquid into her hands—similar to the stuff Macdougal knocked over from the Lab-Top.

Then she flung the liquid into their faces.

Harvey and Macdougal both sputtered as they tried to wipe the liquid from their eyes. Both shuddered and shook.

Did it work?

"Harvey?" Sabrina asked at last.

"Yeah?" he answered.

But the word came from the dog's mouth, not the boy's.

"Darn!"

"Maybe she should just leave it alone," Harvey muttered.

Macdougal turned in surprise. "What?"

Harvey shrugged his reddish-brown shoulders. "I don't know. I guess I've been thinking, and I don't know how to tell you this, Sabrina, but, well, a dog's life is pretty cool. I really sort of like being a dog. Except for the pound business, of course."

"Really?" Macdougal exclaimed. "Diggit! I *love* being a people!"

"Maybe we should just stay switched for a while," Harvey suggested, growing more excited. "After all, this is really the opportunity of a lifetime."

"Rrrradical!" Macdougal agreed.

And then they began to discuss it, completely ignoring the teenage witch who was staring at them as if they'd gone completely mad.

"Whoa there. Wait a minute. *Wait a minute!*" she shouted. "You guys can't do that! Harvey, what about your parents? What about your neighbors? What about school—and *me?*"

I'll never get my Witch's License if anyone finds out about this, she moaned.

"You rang?"

Uh-oh. It couldn't be. This had to be one of the worst times ever for unexpected company.

Especially when that company was your Quizmaster!

☆

Chapter 10

☆

"How's it going, Sabrina Spellman?"

Sabrina's Quizmaster zapped a freeze on her guests, then peered at her through his tiny wire-rimmed sunglasses.

Huh—I'm the one who should be wearing shades, Sabrina thought. His outrageously bright neon-rainbow silk shirt and billowy chartreuse pants were enough to make a chameleon color-blind.

"I hate it when you just pop in like that," she muttered.

"That's my job."

"Maybe you should go into another line of work."

"Now, now, Sabrina," the Quizmaster teased. "Why so grumpy? Could it possibly be because you've mixed up your magic and made a mon-strous mess of things?"

"I have no idea what you're talking about," Sabrina tried, attempting to cover.

The Quizmaster made a face and strolled over to study the statuelike Harvey and Macdougal. "How about that little matter of switching the *very souls* between two of Mother Nature's most innocent creatures—a boy and his dog?"

Sabrina shrugged. "So I had a little accident, that's all. I'm working on fixing everything."

"Good, good." The Quizmaster vanished, then reappeared seconds later sitting cross-legged on top of her dresser.

"Listen, I know I really messed up," Sabrina admitted. "So as long as you're here, how about helping me out?"

The Quizmaster rubbed his chin thoughtfully. "Have you tried the Double Whammy?" he asked.

"Of course."

"Have you tried the Double Whammy with Cheese?"

Sabrina rolled her eyes as the Quizmaster doubled over with laughter.

"Oh, I crack myself up," he gasped.

"Be serious!" Sabrina cried.

"Oh, I am," he told her. "But I can't help you out. Then you'd miss all the fun. And what would you learn if your Quizmaster bailed you out of trouble all the time? You know, I have a wonderful idea," he said, buffing a scuff from his blue suede shoes.

"I can't wait to hear it," Sabrina said sarcastically.

"Let's make this one of your midterm exams," he announced, obviously proud of himself. "Won't that be fun?"

"No, it wouldn't be!" she cried. "You wouldn't!"

The Quizmaster disappeared again, then reappeared by her side. "Sabrina, my dear student. You know I'm only tough on you because I care about your education."

"Thanks a lot."

"My pleasure. And to make things more interesting, I expect you to turn in your work by three o'clock on Saturday."

"Saturday!" Sabrina shrieked. She kicked the foot of her bed in frustration. "That's impossible!"

"Nothing's impossible—if you believe," the Quizmaster said.

"So when did *you* start working at Hallmark?" Sabrina snapped. "Can't you at least give me a clue?"

The Quizmaster looked over the top of his glasses at her. "You're begging me—without even offering chocolate?"

"Poof!" Sabrina zapped up some expensive chocolates in a huge red heart-shaped box. "Candy?" she asked hopefully.

The Quizmaster gratefully took the chocolate. But then he began to fade.

"But what about my clue!" Sabrina shouted.

The Quizmaster grinned mysteriously. "Look in the mirror at your reflection, Sabrina. You'll find all the magic you need." Then, with a jazzy little spin, he disappeared through the wall.

"Thanks a heap, Stressmaster," Sabrina muttered.

"I heard that—*that*—*that* . . ." she heard him yodel from the Other Realm.

Sabrina plopped down on her bed. She was three inches shy of being totally depressed. So she did what she always did when she needed to think.

She ordered pizza. With the works. With a snap of her fingers, it was even faster than guaranteed delivery.

She opened the large cardboard box and reached for a slice, just as she noticed that Harvey and Macdougal were still frozen to the spot.

"Hey, Fizzmaster!" she shouted around a mouthful of extra cheese. "You forgot to undo my friends."

"Sor*rrr*-rrrry," he called over the distance, and seconds later Harvey and Macdougal awoke from their trance.

"Come on, guys, dig in," she said.

She noticed Salem pouting from his spot by the bay window, so she slipped over and secretly zapped him a tiny box of his own. He pawed at the lid and discovered a special treat: tuna and anchovy pizza.

"Thanks," he whispered. "It's the pizza of my

dreams." He nibbled a bite and nearly swooned. "But don't think this makes up for having a dog in the house!"

Just then she heard her aunts come home. Fortunately they used the front door rather than the door to the linen closet this time. And they immediately ran upstairs to check on their favorite niece.

"Oh, how cute!" Hilda said, coming into the room to pat Macdougal on the head. "I've never seen a dog eat pizza before."

Sabrina shrugged. "It's his favorite."

"Hi, Harvey," Aunt Zelda greeted Macdougal the boy. "Did you get your hot-water heater fixed yet?"

"Not yet," Sabrina answered for him.

Zelda folded her arms. "Hmmm, maybe I should—"

"That's okay, Aunt Zelda," Sabrina interrupted, glancing at Harvey. "The water heater guy is coming in the morning. I'm sure he'll be able to fix everything."

"Well, Harvey's welcome to stay as long as it takes," Zelda said graciously. "Just let us know if you need anything."

"Thanks," Macdougal mumbled.

Sabrina was delighted. "Good dog!" she whispered.

"Um, Sabrina," Zelda said sweetly, "could we see you in the hall for a moment?"

"Sure, Aunt Zelda." Her aunts were being so

nice. She wondered if maybe she should just break down and tell them what was going on. Maybe she should ask them for help.

"Sabrina," Zelda said in that stern tone of voice she seemed to save especially for her niece. "I'm more than happy to help Harvey out, but I hope this is not keeping you from studying your handbook. You know how important your Witch's License is. You want to make your father proud, don't you?"

"Of course, Aunt Zelda," she said with a dutiful smile. *Definitely a bad time to tell them,* she decided. "I even talked to Dad about it last night."

"Wonderful! Oh, and Sabrina, I'm afraid Hilda and I have to be out again tonight. The Witches' Council is holding a regional convention. We probably won't be home till dawn. But I installed a new home security system that I ordered from Witch Warehouse that will protect you from all harm—"

"Unless Cousin Amanda decides to show up," Hilda remarked. "Then you're on your own."

"Will you be all right?" Zelda asked.

"I'm fine," Sabrina reassured them. "After all," she added with a laugh, "I've got good old Macdougal to keep me safe."

"He is an adorable dog," Hilda said, dimpling. "Sure we can't keep him?"

"Aunt Hilda, I'm definitely sure."

Once they'd left, Harvey suddenly remembered that he was supposed to call and check in with his parents and the Milligens. He put his front legs on the nightstand, but then his paws knocked the receiver off the phone. "I forgot," he said sheepishly. "Hey, Sabrina, would you mind dialing for me?"

She dialed the phone and then lifted his floppy ear and held the phone up so he could hear. She could hear his parents saying they were having a wonderful time. And how were things back home?

"Well, there's a lot going on," Harvey answered truthfully. "But I'm doing fine."

"Are you coming down with a cold?" his mother asked worriedly. "Your voice sounds different—kind of scratchy."

"No, Mom, I'm fine, really," Harvey said. "I'm just sleepy, I guess."

Then Mr. and Mrs. Milligen wanted Harvey to put Macdougal on the phone. They thought it would be cute to say hello.

Sabrina held her hand over the receiver. "Remember, Macdougal—it's okay to bark, but no English, okay? They might freak out."

Macdougal nodded and answered the phone. He'd listen for a while, then bark. Listen awhile, then bark. When she took the phone back to hang it up, she could hear the Milligens laughing in delight.

"Okay, gang," Sabrina said. "I've enjoyed your . . . uh . . . unusual company, but it's time for bed. And I've got some studying to do."

"Hey, wanna race?" Harvey asked, his paws clicking on the wooden floor as he walked toward the door.

"Diggit!" Macdougal barked.

Scattering throw rugs, they dashed down the hall toward the guest room. *Funny thing*, Sabrina thought. *Those two are really becoming good friends*.

Then she heard Salem's tiny paws hit the floor with a thump. "I suppose I must retire to my duties," he sniffed. "I just hope Macdougal doesn't slobber all over me tonight."

"Hey, it's for a good cause," Sabrina said. "Maybe you can check and see if this qualifies toward all that community service you're supposed to be doing." Community service was part of the Witches' Council's punishment for Salem's world-takeover scam.

"Thanks for reminding me," he said grumpily. "But mind you, hanging out with a dumb dog like this is really bad for my reputation. You'd better figure out something quick, or the fur will fly!"

Chapter 11

☆

Sabrina woke up to brilliant sunshine spilling a rainbow through her stained-glass window.

She stretched quickly. She had the feeling that things were going to work out and it was going to be a wonderful day.

But soon she wondered if she'd gotten up on the wrong side of the bed.

Despite their protests, she tried several ways of switching Harvey and Macdougal back—including one she'd literally dreamed up.

But nothing worked.

So it was back to school for Macdougal the boy. Sabrina hoped things would go more smoothly today, and she planned to keep Macdougal under wraps.

* * *

Good luck!

By the time they got to their lockers, she and Harvey were surrounded. Everyone wanted to talk to "Harvey" about the track meet.

"Just smile and nod and shrug," Sabrina whispered to Macdougal. "That's what the real Harvey would do."

Then Sabrina spotted Valerie in the crowd and waved her over. "Do you have any idea what's going on?" she asked her friend.

"Sure do," Valerie replied with a huge grin. "Guess who's on the front page of the newspaper— hot off the press?" She handed Sabrina a school newspaper. It was covered with a huge photo and story about Harvey Kinkle, rising track star!

"Oh, great," Sabrina mumbled. "I thought it was coming out tomorrow. How'd you get it out so fast?"

"Desktop publishing," Valerie explained. "Plus a twenty-four-hour copy shop."

"You're so dedicated, Val," Sabrina said, trying to smile.

"I thought you'd like it!" Valerie giggled, totally misunderstanding the sentiment behind Sabrina's comment.

Just when they were trying to blend into the woodwork, Macdougal the dog-boy was now surrounded by what he totally didn't need—lots of attention.

In every class kids wished him good luck. Libby and her "popularity" club surrounded him at lunch, blocking him from her view. And when he curled up and took a nap in math class, their teacher whispered, "Shhh! Quiet, everybody. Let's not wake our track star. He needs his sleep!"

At track practice that afternoon the golden retriever in Harvey responded well to all the praise. He ran so well, no one even bothered to ask him why he carried the relay baton in his mouth.

When they came home from track practice, Sabrina decided there was only one thing to do. She gave Harvey and Macdougal baloney sandwiches for a snack and set them down in front of *Mr. Ed* reruns.

Then she ran upstairs and looked up her father in *The Discovery of Magic*.

"Hi, sweetheart!" Edward Spellman exclaimed as his picture shimmered to life. "This is a surprise—two calls in one week."

"Well, I've been studying my Handbook"— which was true—"and I've got this hypothetical question—"

"I'm flattered," her father said. "You've never asked me to help you study before. Hope I'm not too rusty!" He laughed. "However, I must admit I was pretty good in school myself—although there wasn't quite so much to learn five hundred years ago. So, what's the subject?"

"Dogs," she began.

"Dogs? I love dogs! Did I ever tell you about the dog I had for a familiar when I was about your age?

Mother wanted me to get something more acceptable, like a black cat or a phoenix. But no, I wanted a dog. I named him Xanadu, and he was this wonderful black dog who could . . ."

Sabrina listened politely while her father told her all about the tricks he'd taught Xanadu without using any magic at all. *Huh, so my own 100-percent-witch father even likes to do things without magic now and then.*

"Ah, well," her father slowed down at last. "What was it you wanted to ask me?"

"Like I said, it's just a hypothetical question," Sabrina repeated. "You know, for a paper I have to write. If you were to switch the spirits of an animal and a person, and then you wanted to switch them back, how would you do it?"

"Hmmm, now let me think. Perhaps—"

"Sabrina, dear!"

Zelda and Hilda popped in to bring Sabrina some out-of-this-world snacks from the Other Realm.

Sabrina slammed the book shut on her father, who began shouting muffled words, and whirled around. "Hi!"

"Is that Ted?" Zelda asked, reaching for the book.

"We haven't talked to him in *ages,*" Hilda added.

"Um, he said he was in a hurry, he had to go," Sabrina insisted.

"Nonsense," Zelda insisted. She and Hilda managed to wrestle the huge book from Sabrina's arms and opened it to the *S*'s. "He always has time to say hello to his sisters."

The little engraving of her father sprang to life again, and sure enough, just as Sabrina had feared, he resumed answering her "hypothetical" question. "You know, that's one of the things I never did—switch the spirits between a mortal and a dog. I guess I just never really saw the point. Although, now that I think about it, it might have been fun to switch lives with Xanadu and spend a day in a dog's life. How about you two? Any experience performing or reversing such spells?"

"Absolutely not," Zelda said firmly. "And I don't recommend it to—"

"Me, neither," Hilda said. "Why would anyone want to bother—"

Together her aunts' gazes settled on Sabrina. She gulped as she saw the truth dawn on both sisters at exactly the same time.

Her aunts had been practicing the fine art of sibling rivalry for nearly five hundred years, and now they knew each other so well they could practically read each other's minds.

"Ted," Zelda said with forced cheerfulness, "it was *so* good talking with you—"

"But Sabrina needs a little help with her *homework,*" Hilda finished brightly. "Gotta keep up with those studies."

Edward Spellman shook his head in admiration.

"Sabrina is so lucky to have two aunts like you guys, who take such an active interest in her studies. I really appreciate it."

"No problem," Zelda said as she crossed her arms.

"We're happy to do it," Hilda said as she stood with her fists on her hips.

"Uh, love you, Dad," Sabrina said briskly. "Gotta go!"

Slam! Her father's reply was buried somewhere in the pages of the huge book.

Like mirror images, Zelda and Hilda glared at Sabrina with an intensity that could fry chicken. Lightning flashed over their heads.

Sabrina knew she was in hot water. And if she was really lucky, lightning would strike her down before her aunts got their hands on her.

"Penny for your thoughts?" Sabrina said, hoping a little humor might help.

It didn't.

"Sabrina, you *didn't*—" Zelda began.

"Sabrina, you *couldn't*—" Hilda joined in.

"Wait!" Sabrina interrupted. "I know you're going to yell at me, and that's fine, okay, I guess I deserve it, but I'd at least like to point out that it was all an *accident* and that I've been trying for the last two days to figure it out and fix everything back the way it was."

Sabrina took a deep breath. Her only strategy was to throw herself on the mercy of the court.

"Oh, Sabrina, what if the Quizmaster knew about this?" Zelda said.

"Too late," Sabrina admitted. "He already does."

The aunts exchanged a horrified glance.

"What did he say?" they both asked.

"He turned it into an *assignment!*" Sabrina said glumly. "He wouldn't help me one little bit. And I've only got till Saturday afternoon to solve it!"

Now both sisters were smiling. *Uh-oh.*

"Excellent idea," Zelda said.

"What?!"

"It should be a very educational experience," Hilda agreed. She shook her head and sighed. "If I'd had your Quizmaster, I might not have had such a tough time on my finals."

"Believe me," Zelda added, "you'll thank him later."

Sabrina pouted. "Is that all you can say?"

"No, young lady," Zelda shot back. "I have quite a bit more to say. We're very upset with you."

"But it was an accident," Sabrina repeated.

"That's *not* what we're upset about," Hilda said.

Zelda sat down on the bed and took her niece's hand. "Sabrina, it's not the mistakes with the magic that's upsetting. We all make mistakes, especially when we're learning."

"Then why are you mad?" Sabrina asked.

"Number one, you lied to us about what happened with Harvey," Zelda said. "And number two, you didn't come to us to help you when you had a problem."

"But I'm a teenager," Sabrina tried to joke. "Isn't that what I'm supposed to do?"

But Zelda just looked hurt. "I thought, after all this time, that we'd grown closer than that."

Now Sabrina felt really rotten. Her aunts had been so good to her. She was so lucky to have them. "We have," Sabrina insisted. "You two are like my best friends right now, especially since my mom is so far away. But, well . . . I was afraid."

"Afraid of what?" Hilda asked.

Sabrina shrugged. "I don't know. That you'd be mad. That you'd yell at me. That you'd lecture me about studying for my Witch's License." Sabrina realized there was another reason, too. "You guys are so fabulous with your magic. You can do anything! I guess I was also kind of ashamed of the big mess I made. I didn't want you to think I was, you know, magically challenged or something. I even started to tell you once, but you guys were so busy."

Her aunts exchanged an embarrassed glance.

"First of all, Sabrina," Zelda said softly, "we've had hundreds of years to study, and experiment, and practice our magical powers. You've had less than two. You can't expect to be as experienced as we are, or your father."

"Secondly, we apologize for being so busy the last few days," Hilda added. "And we're sorry we come down on you too hard sometimes."

"But it's just because we love you and want you to succeed at becoming a witch," Zelda insisted. "If you don't pass your test when you're eighteen, you'll lose all your witch powers forever. We couldn't bear it if we felt that it was our fault. We'd feel as if we let you—and Ted—down."

Impulsively Sabrina threw her arms around her aunts and hugged them both tight. "I am lucky to have you. And I promise I'll never keep secrets again."

"Well, we'll see about that," Zelda teased. "You are a teenager, after all!"

For the first time in the past two days Sabrina felt the weight of the world lift from her shoulders. It was true what they said: Troubles were easier to bear when you shared them with someone who loved you. She smiled gratefully at her aunts. "So does this mean you'll help me fix it—before Harvey's parents or Macdougal's owners come home?"

"Noooo," Hilda said.

"Definitely not," Zelda agreed.

Sabrina jumped to her feet. "What?"

"We agree with the Quizmaster," Hilda said with a smile. "This will be a wonderful learning experience for you to figure it out by yourself."

"But my deadline's Saturday afternoon!" Sabrina exclaimed.

"My goodness," Hilda said to Zelda. "She's got a whole day and a half to figure it out."

"But what if I can't do it!" Sabrina nearly shrieked.

"Pshaw!" Zelda said as she and Hilda headed for the door. "That's kindergarten stuff. We have a great deal of confidence in you. We know you'll do fine."

"Please!" Sabrina begged. "I need you! Won't you even give me some kind of clue?"

Zelda took Sabrina by the hand and led her to the full-length mirror that hung on her door. "Look in the mirror at your reflection, Sabrina. And you'll find all the magic you need."

"Grrr! I hate all this 'the magic is in you' fluff," Sabrina complained. "I feel like I'm at a motivational seminar for downsized witches!"

Her aunts just laughed and left her to her task.

Sabrina fell back on her bed and stared at the ceiling.

Time was running out!

And she had no idea what she was going to do.

Chapter 12

*W*e love you, Harvey!"

The ninth-grade girls at the end of the hallway giggled, then shyly dashed away around the corner.

Macdougal preened as if he'd just won Best in Show at the New England regional dog show.

Sabrina couldn't believe she had to spend another whole school day walking the dog. She felt like Lassie's bodyguard. People looked right through her—or shoved her out of the way—when they spotted Harvey.

The only break she got was in the girls' room. But even there, she couldn't really escape.

When she stepped inside, the five girls at the mirror stopped brushing their hair. Even Libby Chessler.

"So, Sabrina," a senior named Marissa gushed as

the girls clustered around her, "how's it feel to be dating the star of the track team?"

"Well, Harvey and I aren't really dating," Sabrina explained.

"You could have fooled me," the redhead said.

"Does that mean he's up for grabs for the dance?" Libby asked with a gleam in her eye.

The dance?

There was a dance tonight. Sabrina had totally forgotten. She'd had a few other things on her mind.

"I don't think Harvey's going," she said.

"Not going?" Marissa said. "But he has to. The whole track team will be there. We're going to cheer them on to victory."

Libby dropped her brush into her purse and snapped it closed. "He'll be there," she said. She ran her hand over her dark brown hair, giving it one last look. Then she dashed out of the girls' room like a girl on a mission.

"Uh-oh," Sabrina groaned. "Major disaster."

By the time Sabrina caught up with her runaway dog, Macdougal was smiling as though he'd just been asked out by the most popular girl in school.

"Sabrina!" Macdougal said. "There's a people dance tonight. Why didn't you tell me?"

"Sorry," Sabrina replied. "I forgot. So, do I get the feeling you want to go?"

"Rrrrruf!" Macdougal said. "Who wouldn't?"

"But, Macdougal, you can't!" Sabrina pleaded.

"Libby will take your tender little heart and crush it beneath the granite of her own."

Macdougal got this weird look on Harvey's face, as if he were staring at his own nose. It was the look Harvey often got when he was deep in thought.

"Sabrina," he said at last, "what are you talking about?"

"Aren't you going to the dance with Libby?"

"Libby?" Macdougal grunted. "No way. She smells funny. And she's too bossy." Then he dazzled her with Harvey's lopsided grin. "I'm going with you!"

Sabrina didn't know whether to laugh or cry.

That night, somehow, Sabrina found herself walking into the Westbridge High School gymnasium for a very formal dance. The band was hot, the decorations were cool. And the room was already packed with dancing fools.

Sabrina stepped into the room with a dog who thought he was a boy. Actually, he *was* a boy . . . temporarily. The most popular boy at school.

Maybe this is a dream, Sabrina hoped as she stepped beneath the dazzling strobe lights. *Or maybe some cruel joke that Cousin Amanda is playing on me.*

Macdougal had insisted that they go to the dance.

Harvey had insisted that they go to the dance.

"Why do *you* want me to go to the dance with Macdougal?" she'd asked him in amazement.

"Hey, I'm the guest of honor," Harvey had said. "I gotta be there." He glanced down at his furry paws. "Even if I can't be there. Please, Sabrina?"

Unfortunately for her, she had a soft heart like her dad. So here she was at the big school dance. And her date was a real dog.

Macdougal yanked on her arm as he tried to catch one of the little circles of light.

"Macdougal!" she whispered. "What are you doing?"

"What are those things?" he asked her. "And how do they run away so fast? It's driving me crazy!"

Sabrina rolled her eyes. Then she grabbed Harvey by the chin and made him look up at the ceiling.

"See that big, silvery, spinning ball?" she asked. "The shiny reflectors make these tiny little circles of light sparkle around the room. You can't catch them. They're not things. It's just light."

"Oh." Macdougal seemed pretty disappointed.

But then he spotted the refreshment table.

And in an instant—almost as fast as if they'd traveled by molecular transference—Macdougal had dragged her to the food.

"Mind your manners," she whispered as she held him back from attacking a platter of little sandwiches. "Watch me."

She handed him a paper plate.

His eyes lit up. He started to bite it.

"No!" Sabrina gasped. "It's to put your food on."

"But it's little and flat."

Sabrina took a deep breath and grabbed the plate. She piled it as full of food as she could, then handed it back. "And don't forget to pick up the food with your hands and put it into your mouth," she explained.

Macdougal shrugged. "Seems like an unnecessary extra step, but okay."

He did all right, Sabrina had to admit. He even drank punch without slurping. He was picking up this human stuff pretty fast. Maybe too fast.

But she had to admit, he looked great. After all, he had Harvey's face and body to do it with. They'd dressed him up in Harvey's nice dark suit. And he didn't even mind the tie. He'd said it was a lot more comfortable than the dog collar the Milligens made him wear.

"Hey, Harvey, my man, lookin' good!" Jason Wayne strolled over and gave Harvey some kind of complicated sports handshake. *Where do guys come up with these things?* Sabrina wondered.

Jason glanced appreciatively at the satin dress that Sabrina had "whipped up" at the last minute in the same pale shade of blue as her eyes. "You, too, babe. Totally hot."

"Uh, thanks."

Jason winked at her. "So you two are really back together now, huh?"

"Nope," Sabrina insisted. "Just really good friends."

"Yeah, right." Jason wiggled his eyebrows at her. "Whatever you say, babe."

Then he slapped "Harvey" on the shoulder. "Have a good time with your 'friend,'" he said, laughing as he sauntered off into the crowd.

Suddenly the lights changed to a soft blue, and the band began a slow number. Couples moved onto the dance floor, swaying to the music.

Suddenly Libby appeared, brushing up against Harvey's arm. "So, Harvey, aren't you going to dance?"

Sabrina leaned over. "Harvey doesn't—"

"Sure," Macdougal answered.

Libby smiled smugly, and held up her arm for Harvey to lead her into the crowd.

But instead Macdougal whirled Sabrina onto the floor.

Sabrina stared in surprise as Macdougal did an acceptable version of human dancing. "Where in the world did you learn how to dance?"

"Mrs. Milligen," he said. "She loves music. When I was a little puppy, she used to pick me up and dance me around the living room. It was fun."

"Amazing."

Macdougal frowned. "Sabrina, what do you think dogs do all day? Just lie around?"

"Well, don't you?"

Macdougal thought a moment. "Well, most of the time. But we don't *just* lie there. A lot of times you people just forget we're there. But we're smarter than you think. And we're always watching, looking at things." He spun her around. "You can learn a lot if you keep your muzzle shut and just listen."

"I'm sorry, Macdougal," Sabrina said. "I didn't mean to insult you. And I think you are probably the smartest dog I've ever met."

"Woof," Macdougal said with Harvey's crooked smile.

Most of the evening went by smoothly. Libby and the rest of the cheerleaders led the crowd in a few cheers for the track team.

Suddenly everyone in the gymnasium froze. It reminded Sabrina of the scene in *Sleeping Beauty,* when the fairies put all the members of the kingdom to sleep.

But Sabrina hadn't worked any magic. What was going on?

Then some funky music began to play—even though the band members were as still as a press photo.

Someone tapped her on the shoulder. "May I have this dance?"

Sabrina whirled around—and gulped.

The Quizmaster stood there in a grape-colored tuxedo.

"How's my favorite teenage witch?" he asked cheerfully. "Having fun?"

Sabrina nodded as he gave her a twirl.

The Quizmaster threw himself into some super-funky moves. "How's the midterm going?"

"I'm learning a lot," Sabrina hedged as she tried to keep up with his energetic dancing. *Yeah, right,* she thought, *like all the things that don't work to switch Harvey and Macdougal back.*

"I'm so glad to hear that."

Suddenly he disappeared—

And reappeared at the refreshment table. "Care for some punch? Dancing makes me thirsty."

"No, thanks," Sabrina said.

"Well," he said, "I hate to be a party pooper, but I've got business in the Other Realm. I just wanted to pop in and say 'hi.'"

"And check up on me," Sabrina added.

"Call it what you like." He reappeared beside her and did one final twirl beneath the disco ball. "See you tomorrow . . ." he said as his image disappeared.

An instant later the gymnasium blasted back to life.

Sabrina looked around for Harvey and found him leading a conga line around the dance floor. And when he howled at the moon, he was having so much fun, everyone in the conga line just howled along with him.

But then Coach Tripp went up on the bandstand and picked up the microphone. "I know you're all having a great time," he said. "But I'm going to have to be the bad guy here and send the track team home."

The crowd groaned. Nobody wanted Harvey or the other track team members to leave.

Coach Tripp laughed. "I know, I know. But in case you haven't heard," he joked, "these guys have a big track meet tomorrow. And they need their rest in order to run circles around the other schools. Right?"

"Right!" the crowd cheered. "Go, Fighting Scallions! Go, Fighting Scallions!"

Harvey and all the other athletes waved as they left the gym with their dates.

Sabrina and "Harvey" declined all offers of a ride home. Besides, it was a nice night, and Macdougal liked to walk.

"Thanks, Sabrina," Macdougal said as they headed home.

"For what?"

"For the best night of my life!" he exclaimed, his eyes shining. "And for giving me the chance to be a boy. My life will never be the same again."

Oh, no. He had a funny look on his face. Was he going to try to lick her face again?

But no, he just took her hand.

As they walked through the quiet neighborhoods, underneath the stars, Macdougal suddenly began to whistle.

"Macdougal!" Sabrina said. "Where—"

"I know," he answered with a laugh. "Where in the world did I learn how to whistle like that?"

Sabrina grinned and nodded.

"Hey, people have been whistling at me all my

life!" he said. "And Mr. Milligen? He's the best whistler in the whole wide world. He always whistles when he walks me at night."

Macdougal sighed. "Good old Mr. Milligen. You know, my dad ran off when I was just a pup."

"I'm sorry," Sabrina said softly.

Macdougal shrugged. "It's the way it is in the dog world. But Mr. Milligen—he's been like a father to me."

They walked along in silence for a while. And then Macdougal stopped and held out his long silk tie. "Sabrina?" he asked with a little catch in his voice.

Sabrina smiled and took the end of the tie in her hand. It was a short leash. But it would do.

Then she walked Macdougal all the way home.

And as they walked through the quiet night, a sadness fell over her. She'd totally mixed up the lives of a sweet dog and an even sweeter friend.

And no matter how much fun they were having, it was totally wrong.

Would she ever be able to make things right again?

Chapter 13

☆

☆

Saturday—the day of the regional track meet!

It was about to begin, and Sabrina still hadn't figured out a way to switch Harvey and Macdougal back into their proper bodies.

Not that she hadn't spent half the night trying! She'd tried saying the original magic words backward. She'd tried making up her own magic words. She'd even tried saying them standing on her head and with Harvey and Macdougal back to back.

She'd even admitted to Aunt Zelda that she hadn't put the Lab-Top away properly, and now she wondered if perhaps the chemicals that spilled could have contributed to the mix-up. But when Sabrina helped her aunt identify which chemicals Macdougal had knocked over, Zelda had just laughed. "The only powerful magic in those potions is vitamins. Macdougal spilled distillations I'm developing for creating the perfect multi-fruit-and-vegetable vita-min cocktail shake that's low in fat and calories."

Sabrina felt like giving up. Especially when she saw the huge turnout for the track meet. It was the biggest crowd the track team had ever had. It seemed as if the entire school had shown up. Even Libby and her cheerleaders were there, prancing around with their green and white pom-poms. They'd never managed to grace a track meet with their presence before.

Coach Tripp was smiling as if he'd won the lottery. Vice-principal Kraft was there, looking for student transgressions. And Valerie was running around, snapping pictures for the school paper.

Sabrina had brought both Harvey and Macdou-gal with her to the meet. She was almost out of time! Her deadline with the Quizmaster was 3 P.M., and Harvey's parents and neighbors were due back sometime in the afternoon.

She was going to have to pull off a major miracle before the day was through.

"Hey, Kinkle!" Coach Tripp called out cheer-fully. "Get on over here, big guy. We're ready to warm up!"

Macdougal was psyched. He really responded to the praise he was getting as a major new track star. At home, his owners were very affectionate and quick to praise, but hey, that didn't compare to a stand full of cheering fans!

And the smell of hot dogs and popcorn that filled the stadium.

Reluctantly Sabrina sent him to his coach.

Suddenly she felt something tugging on the bottom of her pants. She glanced down. "Harvey," she whispered, "why are you trying to eat my jeans?"

"I'm not," he whispered back. "I'm just trying to get your attention."

"Okay, you got it. Do you have any ideas?"

"Yes!" Harvey exclaimed. "Whatever you do, don't let your aunt switch me and Macdougal back before the track meet is over."

"But, Harvey, your parents—your neighbors—they'll be here soon."

"Sabrina, I don't care," Harvey said. "It may be Macdougal the dog out there on that starting line. But he's running in Harvey Kinkle's body. It's my reputation on the line. I've gotta win the track meet!"

"But, Harvey—"

"Listen to me, Sabrina. If you switch us back, I know I won't be able to run as fast as Macdougal. I'll lose the meet. If you figure out a way to switch us back now, I'm toast!"

"Yeah," Sabrina said, "but if I don't change you back soon, your parents and neighbors will be back and they'll know something's weird. Then you'll *really* be toast. *I'll* be toast. My Aunt Zelda will be toast, too."

Harvey lay down in the dirt, dropped his head between his paws, and whimpered. "You're right. Either way, I'm toast," he mumbled.

Suddenly the solution "popped up" in Sabrina's head.

Toast!

The toaster in the kitchen!

It all seemed so clear all of a sudden. She could almost see it in her mind like a slow-motion video . . .

When Macdougal crashed into the dining room, Sabrina turned while casting her spell.

It ricocheted off the toaster—which has a mirrored surface!

And then the words from the Quizmaster came back to her:

"Look in the mirror at your reflection, Sabrina. You'll find all the magic you need."

Why hadn't she realized it before? Aunt Zelda had said exactly the same thing:

"Look in the mirror at your reflection, Sabrina. And you'll find all the magic you need."

They'd both given her a clue, and she'd only scoffed at their advice. But now she knew what to do.

She needed to reverse her spell through a *mirror image* to make it work.

But the track meet was about to begin. She'd have to hurry!

Where in the world could she find a mirror at a track meet?

Sabrina searched the field. *There!* A mirrored surface flashing in the sunlight caught her eye. Sabrina shaded her eyes and tried to pinpoint where the reflection was coming from.

Libby Chessler—checking her makeup in a compact right in front of everybody. How tacky. But how lucky!

Sabrina raced down to where the cheerleaders were warming up before the packed bleachers. "Excuse me, Libby?"

Libby whirled around, surprised, her compact held up in the air.

"Thanks!" Sabrina snatched it from her hand.

"Sabrina! You freakazoid!" Libby shouted. "What do you think you're doing?"

"Better save your vocal cords for the meet," Sabrina recommended. "This is an emergency. I'll bring it right back."

Libby stamped her foot in the grass but couldn't chase after her, because the other cheerleaders had begun the first warm-up cheer.

Sabrina's mind was whirring as she ran back toward Harvey the dog. Just wait till she told the Quizmaster about this! Hey, maybe she'd score so many points, she'd get her Witch's License early!

But when she reached the spot beneath the shady tree where she'd left Harvey, he'd disappeared. "Now, where did that dog run off to this time?" she muttered. She glanced around the crowded track area, searching for the familiar golden-red coat.

Uh-oh!

Mr. Kraft had him.

The words from his intercom announcement rang through her head: *"No dogs are allowed on school property. And that means hallways, classrooms, entryways, grounds, and sports fields."*

Mr. Kraft was dragging Macdougal/Harvey away!

Chapter 14

☆

Mr. Kraft!" Sabrina shouted. "Stop!" She ran toward him.

The vice-principal glared at her.

"Uh—sir," she amended.

"I'm kind of busy here, missy. Why don't you make an appointment with the school secretary?"

"But that's my dog," she said, smiling reassuringly at Harvey, who looked kind of nervous. "Well, it's not mine, exactly, I'm just sort of pet-sitting it."

"No dogs are allowed on school property," Mr. Kraft began to recite as he opened the back door to his car. "And that means hallways, classrooms—"

"Yeah, I know, sports fields," Sabrina said. "That's why I'm here. To take him away."

Mr. Kraft tried to shove Harvey into the backseat. "Too late for that. This dog is going to the pound."

"But you can't do that!" Sabrina cried.

Mr. Kraft glared at her again.

"Uh, sir." Sabrina tried to take the leash. "Please, Mr. Kraft, there's no need to bother. I'll just take him home now and everybody will be happy. His owners are due back today. You go on back and enjoy the track meet. I heard we have a good chance to win . . ."

She knew Mr. Kraft was into sports more than just about any other aspect of school—besides rules and punishments, that is. And she saw his eyes linger on the track for a moment, before they snapped back to the matter at hand. "No, ma'am. We are making an example of this dog—and you— so the rest of the students will know I mean business." He peered at Sabrina through his glasses. "Say, you aren't the hooligan who brought a dog to school the other day, are you?"

Sabrina gulped. "No, sir!"

"Are you sure? Isn't Lloyd Krumley's locker near yours?"

Good grief, what does this man do, sit up memorizing locker numbers at night?

"I'm sure," Sabrina said. "Besides, there probably wasn't even a dog in the first place. Lloyd Krumley is so allergic, he was probably sneezing from his new felt-tip pen or something." She chuckled.

Mr. Kraft did not. "Lloyd Krumley happens to be my second cousin's nephew. Once removed."

"Oh. Sorry," she muttered. "It was probably just some dog hair that got on my clothes at home."

But before she could say another word, Mr. Kraft

had locked and slammed the back door, trapping Harvey in the backseat of his car. Then the vice-principal walked around and jumped in the driver's seat.

Harvey whimpered pitifully as he peeked at her through the window, his wet black nose leaving little smudge marks on the window.

"Don't worry!" she mouthed to him as Mr. Kraft jammed the key in the ignition and started the car.

Sabrina didn't know anything about car engines and all those wires and hoses and plugs under the hood. Which was just perfect, since she was using the magic in her fingertip not to fix the car, but to totally wreck it.

RRRRrrrrRRRRrrr—ehhhhhhsssssssss.

The car died.

Spectacularly.

"My baby!" Mr. Kraft shrieked and jumped out to look under the hood.

Sabrina smiled, used magic to quickly unlock the back door, gave Harvey Kinkle the dog a quick little hug, then ran with him over near the starting line of the first race, the 100 meters.

Macdougal the boy stretched Harvey's body up to the sky, then bent into position, with his hands on the ground and his foot pressed against the starting block.

"Harvey," Sabrina whispered to the dog. "Don't ask me to explain it, but I've figured out what to do to change you back. Now run over there and sit next to Macdougal."

"Oh, Sabrina, do I have to?" Harvey yipped,

staring up at her with his gorgeous brown eyes. "I'm just about to become a track star. My name might even go on a plaque in the gym!"

For a moment Sabrina was torn. What a small gift to give a good friend—a chance at fame, however fleeting.

Slam! A car door on the other side of the track snagged her attention.

"Harvey! Look!" she whispered frantically. "It's your parents!"

"Yowl!" he said. "I forgot they were going to try to get back in time for our meet. And Mr. and Mrs. Milligen. I should probably go over to the Milligens first, like a good dog—"

Sabrina knew it couldn't wait. "Sorry, friend. Let's do it!"

Harvey nodded, then dashed toward the body he'd inhabited until two days ago.

"On your mark!" the coach called out.

Sabrina held up the mirror, turning this way and that to get it into position. When the spell ricocheted off the mirror, the angle had to be just right or it would miss Harvey and Macdougal completely.

"Get set!"

Sabrina took a deep breath, repeated the spell backward, then shot her magic into the mirror.

"Go!"

Zap!

Faint stardust sparkled over boy and dog as the ricocheting spell struck them just as Harvey pushed off against the starting block. But no one seemed to notice it in brilliant spring sunlight and the burst of the starter's gun.

And then the runners were off in a burst of speed, grunting, feet churning and arms pumping, along the track toward the finish line.

Sabrina dashed up to the stunned golden retriever, pushing through the crowd that now swarmed around the track. She lost sight of the dog just as the runners closed on the finish line.

And then Sabrina's heart twisted.

A Ridgefield runner had edged past Harvey at the very last second, leaving Harvey to cross the finish line in second place.

"No!" Sabrina cried under her breath.

The cheering crowd moved forward and she spotted the dog, still sitting by the track, shaking his head. He looked up at her.

"Harvey?" She looked back at the runners. The runner in Harvey's body had come in second place after leading the pack. That was incredible!

The Fighting Scallion runner must still be Macdougal in Harvey's body.

The reverse spell mirror magic failed.

And then something even worse happened.

Sabrina saw Harvey's parents rush onto the track to congratulate him.

How long would it take for them to figure out their son was a dog?

... ...

Chapter 15

Woof! Woof!" The dog beside her began barking madly, straining at the leash.

"Yeah, Harvey, I know. It didn't work," Sabrina said. "But don't worry, I'll keep working on it. And I promise you I'll figure something out."

But Harvey wasn't listening to her. He just kept pulling on the leash, trying to drag her toward the end of the track, where Harvey's parents and Mr. and Mrs. Milligen had gathered.

"Harvey," Sabrina said. "Are you sure you're ready to face this? Harvey? Harvey!"

"Sabrina!" Libby Chessler said, walking past her toward the Gatorade stand. "Why in the world are you calling that dog Harvey?"

Oops. Sabrina glanced up at the nosy cheerleader. Her two best friends, Jill and Cee Cee, flanked her like a couple of bookends, imitating her repulsed expression as if they'd been practicing it in front of the mirror.

"Because—" Sabrina shrugged. "Never mind. Oh, and here's your mirror back. Thanks a lot."

Libby glared at it as if it were contaminated with cooties. "Eww. No, thanks. You can keep it. I don't want to get freak germs on me." She glanced at her friends with a self-satisfied grin. "The condition might be contagious!"

She and her friends laughed as they walked off, but Sabrina couldn't care less. It was ridiculous to work up a sweat over Libby's lame games when there were problems like souls inhabiting the wrong bodies to deal with.

Suddenly Harvey yanked so hard on his leash that Sabrina dropped the end, and the dog shot across the track toward disaster.

Taking a deep breath, Sabrina ran after him. She was pretty sure these guys would need a little help keeping things under control.

As she neared the group of adults surrounding the boy that they all thought was Harvey, she winced as she overheard scraps of conversation.

"Harvey, you were magnificent!" his father was saying, slapping his son on the back.

"We're so proud of you!" his mother said, giving him a great big hug.

"Macdougal!" Mrs. Milligen squealed as the dog jumped up into her arms. "Hello, sugar baby, we missed you so much!"

Too bad everybody was hugging the wrong loved one!

But then Macdougal turned to Sabrina, grabbing both her hands in his. "Sabrina!" he exclaimed, panting hard. "I did it! I really did it!"

"I know, you were great," she began, then peered closely into his eyes. "Harvey?"

"Of course it's Harvey," his father laughed. "Who else would it be?"

And then Harvey gave her a hug so he could whisper in her ear. "It's me, Sabrina. It's really me. I'm back in my own body."

"Harvey? Really?" She stared into his eyes. "But how did you do it?" she whispered. "When I saw you cross the finish line so fast, I thought the spell—" She coughed suddenly to cover up her slip. "I mean the switch didn't work. How'd you do it?"

"Well, I have been working out pretty hard at track this year anyway," he said. "But—I don't know, I can't explain it exactly. These days as a dog, I did a lot of running around. And somehow— it's like some of Macdougal's natural instincts, or his running tricks—or something!—stayed with me. It's like I knew how to run *better!*"

Harvey bent down on one knee to give Macdougal a big hug. "Macdougal," he said, "you're the greatest dog in the world. I'll never forget this."

Macdougal happily licked Harvey's face.

"Forget it?" Mr. Milligen said. "How could you forget it? We only live next door. And hey—it's obvious Macdougal really likes you. Think you'd be interested in dog-sitting next month?"

"Sure," Harvey said. "Any time. But how come?"

"How come?" Mr. Milligen looked at Mr. Kinkle, and then all the grown-ups burst out laughing.

"Because we and your parents are such excellent bowlers that next month we're going to the nationals!"

"All right!" Harvey shouted. "Well, I guess I gotta get back. I've got several more events—and man, am I psyched!"

Sabrina's heart soared to see Harvey so happy. He might not come in first in every race today, and the Fighting Scallions might not ace the meet without Macdougal as a secret weapon. But any fame Harvey earned today would be won with his own two feet. And she knew that would make him far happier than any false glory.

Harvey turned to Sabrina and gave her a wink. "Thanks again, Sab. Meet me at the Slicery after the meet?"

"I'll be there," she promised, "with all the rest of your fan club!"

Harvey laughed and squeezed her arm. Then he was jogging confidently toward his teammates.

Sabrina said good-bye to Harvey's parents and the Milligens, then wandered back to the bleachers to see if she could find Valerie, when suddenly she felt someone appear right behind her.

"A-plus, Sabrina Spellman," the Quizmaster

said in a low conspiratorial voice. He glanced at his watch. "Assignment completed, with three minutes and forty-seven seconds to spare."

"Whoo-hoo!" Sabrina cheered. But then she quit smiling and stared at her instructor. "What in the world are you wearing?"

The usually flamboyant dresser glanced down at his dowdy duds. He was wearing a plain brown shirt, gray-brown pants, and scuffed loafers.

"Loafers?" Sabrina said in disbelief. "And hey, your baseball cap doesn't even have a logo on it. What gives?"

"Shhh," the Quizmaster scolded, glancing suspiciously left and right. "I'm traveling incognito today. You see, I'm rather fleet of foot myself, and I thought I might stick around and catch the rest of the track meet with you. If that's okay with you?"

"Absolutely," Sabrina said. She led him to a seat at the top of the bleachers, where she'd be sure to see Harvey's every move. Once seated, she zapped a cell phone into her hands behind her back, then called her aunts to give them the good news: Harvey and Macdougal were back to normal, Harvey was doing great at the meet, and she'd passed the Quizmaster's test with flying colors.

"Oh, Sabrina, we knew you could do it!" Aunt Zelda exclaimed happily. "You're going to make a wonderful witch."

"Thanks, Aunt Zelda," she replied. "And I think you're right, I just might—*if* I keep listening to you and Aunt Hilda."

When she hung up, she asked the Quizmaster, "Do you think we'll have a problem in the future with Harvey? You know, questioning this whole experience? I mean the explanation I gave him about Aunt Zelda's experiments is kind of far-out."

"Hey, these people watch the *X-Files*. They'll believe anything." The Quizmaster shook his head. "Nah. Mortals—no offense, now—"

"None taken."

"Mortals have a way of rationalizing everything. Of finding ways to make things make sense. They have trouble dealing with things they don't understand. Who knows? As time passes, Harvey may even begin to doubt what happened. He may try to tell himself it was all a dream."

Suddenly Sabrina jumped up as Harvey tore into another race. "Whoo-hoo!" she shouted, waving a fist in the air. "Go, Harvey!" She shook her head in amazement as she watched her friend run. "Maybe so. But I don't think he'll ever forget what it feels like to run like a dog off a leash.

"By the way," Sabrina said as she sat back down. "Do I get extra credit for being nice to you?"

"I should say yes," her instructor said with a grin. "But no, not really."

"Oh, well." She turned away from the crowd for a moment. A brief colored light flashed. And when she turned around again, she was holding a covered plate that smelled like chocolate.

"Care for a brownie?" she asked.

"Uh-*huh*—as long as it's chocolate." The Quizmaster took a gargantuan bite and moaned in delight. "Absolutely divine. Sabrina Spellman, I may have to rethink that extra credit issue after all. Where *did* you ever get this recipe?"

"It's my Granny's recipe," she said. "An old-fashioned favorite from my mother's side. Just baked a brand-new way."

The Quizmaster nodded his head. "It's a winner."

"Mmmm-hmm!" Sabrina agreed as she bit into one herself.

About the Author

Cathy East Dubowski has known and loved many dogs in her lifetime, including Sleepy, who wasn't; Lady, who wasn't, either; Neil, named after Neil Armstrong, the first man on the moon; and Falstaff, a country dog who took a big bite out of the Big Apple. But her favorite of all is the real Macdougal, who was the inspiration for the dog in this story (and whose picture appears on the cover). A reddish-brown golden retriever, Macdougal bravely guards the Dubowski household against dangerous FedEx and UPS employees and other stray strangers, who don't know his secret: that he's actually the most affectionate dog that was ever born.

Macdougal asked the author to say that if more people could switch places with dogs for a few days—the way Harvey Kinkle does in this story—the world might be a better place.

Cathy has written many books for kids, including another *Sabrina the Teenage Witch* book, *Santa's Little Helper;* the Secret World of Alex Mack books *Cleanup Catastrophe!, Take a Hike!, Bonjour, Alex!,* and *Truth Trap!,* published by Archway Paperbacks; plus several in the Full House/Michelle series, published by Minstrel Books. One of her original books for younger readers, *Cave Boy,* a collaboration with her husband, Mark Dubowski, a cartoonist and illustrator, was named an International Reading Association Children's Choice.

Cathy and Macdougal live in North Carolina, where he enjoys chasing squirrels and begging table scraps from the Dubowski daughters, Lauren and Megan. Cathy is currently collaborating with her husband, Mark, on another Alex Mack book plus a story for The Mystery Files of Shelby Woo.

THE HOTTEST STARS
THE BEST BIOGRAPHIES

☆ **Hanson: MMMBop to the Top** ☆
By Jill Mattthews

☆ **Hanson: The Ultimate Trivia Book!** ☆
By Matt Netter

☆ **Isaac Hanson: Totally Ike!** ☆
By Nancy Krulik

☆ **Taylor Hanson: Totally Taylor!** ☆
By Nancy Krulik

☆ **Zac Hanson: Totally Zac!** ☆
By Matt Netter

☆ **Jonathan Taylor Thomas:
Totally JTT!** ☆
By Michael-Anne Johns

☆ **Leonardo DiCaprio: A Biography** ☆
By Nancy Krulik

☆ **Will Power!
A Biography of Will Smith** ☆
By Jan Berenson

☆ **Prince William:
The Boy Who Will Be King** ☆
By Randi Reisfeld

Available from Archway Paperbacks
Published by Pocket Books

1491

Put a little magic in your everyday life!

Magic Handbook

Patricia Barnes-Svarney

Sabrina has a Magic Handbook, full of spells
and rules to help her learn to control her magic.
Now you can have your own Magic Handbook,
full of tricks and everyday experiments you
can do to find the magic that's inside and all
around you!

From Archway Paperbacks
Published by Pocket Books

2021-01

What's it like to be a Witch?

Sabrina
The Teenage Witch™

"I'm 16, I'm a Witch, and I *still* have to go to school?"

◆◆◆◆◆

Based on the hit TV series
Look for a new title every other month.

From Archway Paperbacks
Published by Pocket Books

1345-08